ALL THE EMPTY PLACES

**To celebrate eighteen years
of Crime and Noir Fiction publishing,
No Exit Press is reissuing 18 of its classic titles
in special numbered and limited editions**

www.noexit.co.uk/18

Titles by the same author

Quick Before They Catch Us

ALL THE EMPTY PLACES

Mark Timlin

NO EXIT PRESS

For Ion

First published by No Exit Press in 2001
This edition published 2005 by No Exit Press
P.O.Box 394, Harpenden, Herts, AL5 1XJ
www.noexit.co.uk/18

ISBN 1 84243 164 1

New setting by Avocet Typeset, Chilton, Aylesbury, Bucks
Printed and bound in Great Britain by Cox & Wyman, Reading

Two people won't be around to read this book, and I miss them. So, I'd just like to remember Pam Smith & Les Green.
Rest in Peace both of you.

May God stand between you and harm
in all the empty places you must walk
Ancient blessing

Prologue

BLOOD.

First thing to do was to wash the blood off my hands. Blood and the filth ingrained into my skin and under my fingernails. So much blood and dirt that I thought I'd never get clean again. And maybe I won't.

But that's my problem. And even after I'd showered for the third time and the water was running cold I still felt dirty.

At least I'm here and I'm alive when so many aren't, mostly by my hands, so that when I look down at them I know that I'll always be able to see the shadows of the blood there as long as I live.

Blood, yes, but guilt no. I cleaned a house that needed cleaning. I cleared out a nest of rats, and if I'm not exactly proud of what I did, I feel no regrets. The world's a better place for what happened. At least that's what I keep telling myself.

And the money. I'd never seen so much money in my life. And jewels. A king's ransom. A cliché, but true. Diamonds, rubies, pearls, sapphires, emeralds, the light sparkling on their facets and gold settings until they almost blinded me. And coins too. Sovereigns and Krugerrands that had been almost too heavy to bring out, dragging the heavy bags along behind me through mud and shit and so close to being shot or drowned or caught except for the two explosions that shook the streets and blew all the cables that fed the CCTV cameras . . .

But I'm getting ahead of myself.

And the rain that night. I'll never forget that rain. More rain than the sewers could cope with. Like a monsoon beating down on London, with lightning coming from the four corners of the compass making the streets as bright as the brightest day. Fork and sheet, with the thunder so loud it matched the explosions that demolished at least one building and saved me. Then loading up the Jaguar and driving away whilst the police and fire fighters and anyone else in a uniform with a car or truck with a rotating light on top ran about like chickens minus heads. And even then nearly being captured by a bunch of nosy cops, but getting away by the skin of my teeth.

Then back home to unload the car and take it up to a quiet spot and douse it in petrol and set it on fire leaving no clues. At least I hope no clues. But the best laid plans of mice and men . . .

Not that there'd ever been a plan. Not *my* plan anyway. Someone else's. But the plan had been screwed from the start, and circumstances forced me to get involved, and the plan had fallen apart as so many plans do.

And after I torched the car, back to the silence of my flat and the one bag I'd carried inside with me, as much as anything to prove that it had all been real, not just some crazy dream. Back to empty it onto my bed and look at the money and the jewels and the coins, my only companion an old teddy bear who sits on the corner of the bed and squints myopically at me through beady eyes that look in two directions at once. My only companion apart from the inevitable bottle that was waiting patiently there for me, and a packet of Silk Cut bought on the walk home through a purple summer dawn with just the faintest tinge of autumn in the air, and once there, a salute to Teddy with a full glass, and light a cigarette with a fifty pound note, one of thousands, that won't be missed, by me at least, although someone else will and curse me and the rest of them.

But the rest of them don't exist any more.

There's just me and Teddy and so much money and other stuff that I'll never have to lift a finger again as long as I live, and there'll still be plenty left over. That is if the police don't come.

And even if they do I couldn't give a shit. Because she's not here with me. Just me and Teddy, and Teddy never says a word no matter how hard I listen.

And believe me I listen. All through that day and the interminable days that follow.

That was the end.

But it was different in the beginning.

Part One

Sheila

Part One

Suicide

One

IT'S FUNNY HOW some days start off one way and end another, and something as insignificant as a pint of milk can change your life for ever.

That particular Sunday morning I woke up with nothing more on my mind than how to get through the most boring day of the week. I fancied a cup of tea but the milk in the fridge had gone off. Nothing new there then.

Sod it, I thought and looked at my watch. Ten to twelve and the streets were well aired, so I pulled on a cleanish sweatshirt that didn't smell too bad, jeans and loafers and left the house. I hadn't shaved and had just run a comb through my hair so I looked a bit of a state, but then it was Sunday and there was no one around to see me, or for that matter, care if they did see.

It was spring. A particularly mild one that year, and the almond and cherry trees were in full flower in the front gardens as I walked down towards the main street, their pink and white flowers haloing the trees and dropping gently to the pavement to make a carpet for me to walk on. It was beautiful that Sunday, but I hardly noticed. It's that time of the year again now and as I gaze out of my window those same trees are in bloom once more. I notice their beauty now, but I'm alone and have no one to share that beauty with. You might say that's the story of my life.

I went into the newsagent at the bottom of my road, bought a *Sunday Times*, twenty Silk Cut and the milk, paid up and left. I stopped outside long enough to glance at the headlines on the front page, which concerned some minister of the Crown caught red handed with his fingers in the till, when someone called my name. I looked up and saw her walking out of the little minimarket two doors down from the newsagent. She was carrying a carton of milk too. 'Snap,' I said and held up mine.

'Bloody nuisance isn't it?' she said. 'Running out.'

'Yeah,' I replied. 'Can't get started without my cup of tea.'

'Just getting started eh? Shame on you.'

For some unknown reason I felt guilty and started to explain. 'It is Sunday,' I said. 'And I didn't have much on.'

'I can see that from your immaculate grooming,' she said. 'I assumed you weren't just back from church.'

I felt guilty again and rubbed my hand across my hair. 'It just didn't seem worth it for a bit of shopping,' I explained.

She grinned. 'I know,' she said. 'You don't have to apologise to me. I'm exactly the same, always scruffy on a Sunday.'

She looked pretty good for scruffy and I said so.

'Yeah, sure,' she replied. 'So how have you been?'

'Not bad. You?'

She wrinkled her nose. 'Not too good. You know Johnny's gone.'

'I heard,' I said. Johnny Tufnell was her long time boyfriend. A right little snake in the grass. Petty crook, small time drug dealer and general ruffian for hire for anyone with enough money and little regard for law and order. How she'd gone out with him in the first place I'd never known, let alone stay with him for what must have been half a dozen years, visiting him on his stays in various penal institutions up and down the country carrying treats to make him happy, keeping their home going when he was gone and watching him fuck up every time he got out. And I suspected he was a bit fisty with it when he'd had a few. I'd seen her some mornings on her way to work with a shiner disguised by dark glasses and heavy make-up, but it was her life and if she wanted to run it like she was a punch bag for Johnny to take out his frustrations on, it was her choice, and certainly I had never run my life well enough to be able to interfere. Her name was Sheila. Sheila Madden. And I often wonder what would have happened if one of us had decided to go out for milk ten minutes earlier or later on that particular spring Sunday morning.

The reasons I knew her were twofold. First, she worked for a geezer called Jerry Finbarr, a well bent brief for half of south London's villains, who had a poky office in Brixton, a massive mansion in Bromley where he kept his wife and two kids, and a little pied-à-terre in Herne Hill where he entertained his mistresses of various hues and sexual persuasions. I'd had some need of Jerry's professional services myself from time to time and had met Sheila at the office where she typed out briefs, answered the phone and made coffee for all and sundry. And then I discovered she lived just round the corner from me in a little flat on the edge of the council estate with Johnny when he was out of jail, and alone when he wasn't. From time to time I'd bump into her in the local pub we shared and we'd have a drink and talk about mutual acquaintances of the dodgy kind, and have a laugh and say goodbye and that was that. There was nothing there, even though she had the kind of looks that make me shiver. Not exactly drop dead gorgeous, but interesting, with a vulnerability that made me want to wrap her up and make sure she was safe and warm. It was a simple case of chemistry. She was the kind of woman who made the minutes fly by when you were with her and drag after she'd gone. But she was Johnny Tufnell's woman and I didn't fancy getting involved. Not that Johnny himself worried me, but he had enough nutty mates who wouldn't mind waiting outside my door with crowbars and baseball bats, and if I'm going to go in for cosmetic surgery I'd prefer it was by choice rather than necessity.

She looked at her watch. 'What are you doing now?' she asked.

'Like I said, nothing,' I replied. 'Read the paper, watch some TV. It's Sunday.'

'You keep saying that.'

I nodded agreement. I did keep saying that, and I felt about sixteen and never been kissed.

'Pub's open,' she said. 'Just. Are you sure you need that tea, or would you prefer something stronger?'

I was surprised at the invitation. Surprised and to be honest a bit excited. It was just another bloody Sunday with no one to talk to and nothing to do and I couldn't think of anyone I'd rather be with. 'Alright,' I said. 'Come on then.'

'Just a quick one,' she said. 'Then I'll have to go.'

'Whatever,' I said, and we crossed the road and pushed open the door of the pub that the barman had just unlocked and joined the two or three hardened regulars waiting to be served.

I ordered a pint of lager for myself and a G&T, ice and slice for her, and we took them and our meagre shopping to a table in the corner. 'Well, Sheila,' I said when I'd lit cigarettes from my new packet for both of us, 'what's shaking with you?'

'Not much. Work as usual, freezer food and TV at night.'

It sounded depressingly like my life except that I wasn't working. I had a few quid and not much energy so that was that.

'Still slaving for Finbarr?' I said.

She nodded.

'So what's the skinny?' I asked. 'Anything juicy in the pipeline?'

'You know I can't talk about that,' she replied. 'It might be someone you know.'

'Wouldn't be much fun if it wasn't,' I said.

She grinned again. 'What about you?' she asked.

'Nothing exciting,' I said. 'Semi-retirement you might call it.'

'It's alright for some.' She stubbed out her half finished cigarette. 'I need to pee,' she said, got up and headed for the ladies.

I watched her as she went. She was smallish and blondish, although I reckoned the colour was out of a bottle and that made me wonder what her real hair colour was, and I've discovered there's only one way to find out and that's not always sure fire. She was wearing a dark red fake furry jacket over a black sweater, cream coloured jeans and platform soled black boots with thin heels. Real ankle breakers I reckoned as I scoped the roll of her backside as she walked. She had a great arse, round but not too sloppy. I like a woman with curves and I scratched at my stubble and flattened my hair with my hand again. Just my luck, I thought. To look a mess when I run into an attractive woman. Then I smiled. Jesus, I thought. Who are you kidding? Fat chance. But it had been a long time since I'd been with a woman. Too long, and the memories weren't the greatest. Another reason I hadn't tried it on with Sheila was because, once, a long time ago, she'd told me that she was a one man woman. She didn't fuck around when she was involved, and I remembered thinking that it was a shame she'd been involved with such a scumbag as Johnny Tufnell and left it at that.

When she came back and joined me I said, 'So what happened to Johnny then?'

Her face hardened behind fresh make-up. 'Fuck knows,' she said. 'And I couldn't care less.'

I'd never heard her swear before and I figured that whatever had happened it had been rough. 'Is he back inside?' I asked.

She shook her head. 'Not as far as I know. Leastwise he hasn't been to see Finbarr lately.'

'Maybe he's going straight,' I said.

'Have you seen many pigs flying round here lately?'

'Not a lot,' I said, glancing out of the window which made her laugh. I liked that – making her laugh.

'And you?' she asked. 'What happened to your girlfriend? Melanie wasn't it?'

I was surprised she remembered. 'That's right,' I said. 'History.' Mel had packed her bags and gone a long time previously. Last I'd heard she'd found someone to match her expectations. I knew it would never be me. The story of my life in a lot of ways again. I'd wished her good luck as I'd waved her goodbye. There was nothing else for me to do.

'Sorry,' said Sheila.

'Don't be. It wasn't meant to happen. She wanted me to change, I wanted her not to. It's a recipe for disaster.'

'I wish I'd realised that about me and Johnny when I met him. It would've saved me years of grief.'

'Sometimes you know these things, sometimes you don't.'

'And sometimes you're just plain stupid like me.'

'Don't run yourself down. From what I heard you did your best.'

'You've talked about me then.'

I was embarrassed again. 'Just pub talk, you know what I mean.'

'Yeah. It's nice to know I'm the subject of public bar gossip. Makes me feel wanted.'

'Saloon,' I said.

'What?'

'Saloon bar gossip. You're much too classy for the public.'

I could've lost her then, but instead she laughed again. It wasn't such a happy laugh and I suddenly felt sorry for her being stuck with that bastard for so long and knowing people were talking about her. 'Sorry,' she said. 'Sometimes I take myself too seriously.'

'Sometimes you have to, otherwise life has a habit of running away with you.'

'Bit of a philosopher, Nick?'

'Only in pubs.'

'And only in the saloon bar.'

'That's right.'

'You don't seem to take things seriously,' she said. 'From what I've seen of you.'

'You'd be surprised.'

'Wouldn't be the first time.'

'So what are you doing later?' I asked, changing the subject.

'Washing my smalls.'

I wished she hadn't said that as it set me thinking about all sorts of things again. Like what she was wearing underneath her sweater and jeans for instance. 'Nothing urgent then?'

'You haven't seen the state of my knicker drawer.'

There she was, doing it again. 'No,' I said, 'I haven't'

'Why?' she asked.

'I just wondered if you fancied some lunch?'

'Might do. You buying?'

'Might do,' I said.

'Alright then. Where shall we go?'

Two

WE ATE AT the Pizza Express just a few hundred yards down the road. It was cheap and cheerful. Although I'd told Sheila I was in semi-retirement it didn't mean I was on a pension. Far from it. She had a Four Seasons, I had an American. We drank a carafe of house red with the meal followed by coffees and brandies. I enjoyed the food and her company. Over the second brandy she said, 'Pretty good.'

'You'll always get a warm welcome at Pizza Express.'

'Is that so?'

'Goes with the territory.'

'If you say so.'

'I do.'

'I've enjoyed myself today, Nick.'

'Me too.'

'Why haven't we ever done this before? You just living around the corner and all?'

'I don't know. It could have something to do with Johnny.'

'Oh yes, Johnny. It all comes back down to him doesn't it.'

'He was your boyfriend.'

'What a quaint, old-fashioned term.'

'I'm just a quaint, old-fashioned kind of guy.'

'Are you?'

'I like to think so.'

'And I got stuck with a bastard.'

Some women seem to prefer them, I thought, but decided it was better to keep the thought to myself. 'But you're rid of him now.'

'It took a long time.'

'But better late than never.'

'I'll drink to that,' she said, and we clinked glasses. 'I've got a bottle of wine at home,' she said when she'd emptied her glass. 'Fancy a drop?'

'I thought you had an appointment with your underwear and the washing machine.'

'That was just in case you were boring.'

'I'm never boring.'

'Everybody's boring sometimes,' she replied. 'But so far you've been OK.'

'Thank you so much,' I said.

'So do you want to come back for a drink or not?'

I was feeling good so I said, 'Sure. The offie's still open, I'll get a bottle too.'

'Sounds like we're in for a long afternoon,' she remarked. 'And we only came out for milk.'

'If you don't want to . . .' I didn't finish the sentence.

She smiled, and not for the first time I clocked that she had a lovely mouth. And green eyes. I'm a sucker for green eyes. 'Course I do,' she said. 'Just don't expect any extras to be on the menu.'

'I never do,' I said. And that was the truth.

'Come on then,' she said, and I paid the bill and we left. On the way back we stopped off at the off licence for a bottle of decent red for me and cigarettes for her.

We strolled up the road towards her house, walking apart, and although I wanted to take her arm or hold her hand I didn't.

She let us in to her house and we went up to her flat, which was a top half conversion and where I'd never been before. As we went through her flat door I caught the whiff of fresh paint.

'I just decorated,' she said. 'Get rid of the remains of Johnny.'

'Sounds fair,' I said. 'Got a bottle opener?'

'In the top drawer on the left in the kitchen. Glasses are up top. Second cupboard in.'

Whilst I got the necessary she turned on the stereo.

Sticky moment. What if she was a Dire Straits fan?

But she wasn't. Or at least she didn't spoil the moment by choosing one of their albums. Instead she put on a Tamla Motown compilation of sixties hits and turned the volume down, which suited me just fine.

I poured out the wine to the accompaniment of Martha and the Vandellas and sat on the sofa in the living room where she was perched on the matching armchair. The room faced west into the afternoon sun which shone through the open curtains and made the atmosphere cosy and pleasant. We clinked glasses and drank, and she said, 'I think I'm getting a bit pissed.'

'It's Sunday,' I said. 'What else are Sundays for?'

'You and your bloody Sundays,' she said. 'Can't you talk about anything else?'

'Getting boring am I?' I asked.

'No,' she said. 'Sorry, that was mean. And you're right. I'm just not used to having fun.'

'You should get used to it,' I said. 'It's good.'

'It's good with you,' she said, and the words hung heavy in the warm air in the room.

'And you too,' I said in to the silence that followed.

'You don't know me.'

'I know you well enough.'

'Not true,' she said.

'If you say so,' and I filled her glass again and we toasted each other once more, and I realised she wasn't the only one getting a bit merry and bright that afternoon.

Around six we'd finished both bottles of wine and were making a big dent in a bottle of Greek brandy that she'd found in the sideboard and told me was a souvenir of the last holiday she'd taken with Johnny. Even with the connotations it tasted just terrific and the music had gone from Motown to Blue Note via some Bluegrass collection. 'Jesus,' she said, 'but I have to go to the loo again.' And she left me still sitting on the sofa and staggered out of the room banging her shoulder on the door post as she went.

There was an old stuffed teddy bear with a wonky eye on the table and I reached over and picked it up. 'Well Teddy, what do you reckon?' I said. 'What kind of situation have we found ourselves in here?' But not a word did he say in reply. After a few minutes with no sign of her I started to worry. I was totally drunk by then and I thought she might be ill. 'Come on Teddy,' I said. 'Let's go look.'

I went out to the bathroom and knocked on the door. There was no reply. Shit, I thought. What now? I rapped harder, and when I was still met by silence I tried the door. It was open. Sheila was sitting on the toilet with her jeans and knickers pulled down over her thighs. Two questions were immediately answered. She was wearing black underwear and her true hair colour was British mouse. She looked up at me as I stood in the doorway clutching Teddy in my hand. 'Are you OK?' I asked. 'I was getting worried. Sorry. I didn't mean to burst in. I knocked.' It sounded pretty lame and I felt pretty stupid.

'Just had to pee. Have I been long?'

'Yeah. I thought you might be being sick.'

She giggled and shook her head. 'No. Just thinking.'

'Fine,' I said.

'What are you doing with Teddy?' she asked.

'Nothing. I just thought . . .' I stopped.

'What?'

'That you wouldn't be scared of me coming in if I was carrying a furry animal.'

She laughed out loud at that. 'Christ, Nick,' she said. 'There's some furry animals you could have in your hand that would scare me, but you're right. Teddy doesn't. I've got to lie down. I'm out of it. Help me up.'

I dropped Teddy into the dry bath next to where she was sitting and she caught my hand and I pulled her upright. She was unsteady on those damned heels and fell against me and I held her as she pulled up her

pants and jeans. She didn't seem in the least concerned
that I'd caught her on the toilet, so that was alright.
'Bedroom's past the living room,' she said and leant on
me as I half walked half carried her there. 'Damn. But I
haven't been this pissed in ages,' she said as she dropped
onto the bed.

'You going to be alright?' I said.

'Sure.'

'I'll get off then.'

'No,' she almost wailed and held out her hand. 'Stay.'

I didn't know what to do. 'You're drunk,' I said. 'You
need to sleep.'

'I'll sleep better with you here.'

'I can't.'

'Why not?'

There was no reason. 'You'll regret it in the morning,'
I said weakly. But I wanted to stay. I hadn't slept with a
woman for months, and the more of Sheila I saw the more
I wanted her. Or at least not to leave her. Just stay close
and hold her.

'Please don't go,' she said. 'I get lonely.'

Christ, Sheila, don't we all, I thought, as she awkwardly
pulled off her boots and socks, jeans and sweater to reveal
a black bra that matched her knickers. 'Just promise me
one thing,' I said as I watched her.

'What?'

'Promise you won't go weird on me later.'

'I promise,' she said, but I didn't really believe her.

I stripped down to my T-shirt and shorts and she
grinned wickedly. 'So that's what you wear,' she said.

'That's it,' I agreed and we both climbed under the
duvet and I held her in the silence that reigned in the
flat after the CD had finished.

We kissed then, in the darkness of the room with the
curtains drawn, and our tongues met almost shyly. We
held each other very close like a pair of orphans who'd
found a family to belong to.

ALL THE EMPTY PLACES   19

We were both too drunk to get into any grand pro-
ductions then, but there's an awful lot of fun to be had
just touching and stroking and kissing, even though I'm
sure we both passed out at least once. But it wasn't a
staying awake contest, or even a sex contest, just two
sparks of humanity who by luck had bumped into each
other at the right time and place. I helped her out of
her bra and her breasts were full and round and soft
with nipples the colour and length of pencil erasers and
I kissed them gently. Her skin was like silky velvet, soft
and warm, and I drank in the smell of her as eagerly
as I'd drunk the wine earlier. 'You're lovely,' I whis-
pered.
She shook her head. 'Don't say that,' she said. 'I don't
like it.'
'Why not?'
'I don't relate to compliments. I'm not used to them.
Johnny knocked that bit out of me.'
'With his fists?'
'And his tongue. He was very cruel.'
'He didn't deserve you.'
'Oh I think he did. He deserved me just fine. We were
made for each other.'
'No.'
'Nick.'
'What?'
'Shut up and kiss me some more.' And I imagine that's
when I started to fall in love with her.
At around nine I got up and found a bottle of Evian
water in the fridge, turned off the stereo that was hum-
ming quietly to itself in the corner and went back to bed
with cigarettes and the ashtray. 'My mouth tastes like shit,'
said Sheila as we shared a cigarette and the bottle and after
I'd stubbed it out we both fell asleep.
I woke up at four in the morning and pushed my fingers
into her pants to wake her, and we had another go. But we
were still half pissed although I like to think I made her

come before falling asleep again. But that might just be a bloke thing.

I woke again at six and she was sitting up in bed looking at me. I felt that something had changed

'Surprise,' I said to break the silence.

'You're here.'

'Looks like it. Is something wrong?'

She shook her head. 'Did we?'

'You've still got your knickers on,' I said. 'And they've stayed on.'

'Why not?'

'We were both too drunk,' I said. 'I thought maybe it wasn't the right time. I thought it would be taking advantage.'

'Did I want to?'

What a question. 'I don't know.'

'Did you want to?'

'Yes.'

'Do you think I'd've let you?'

I was beginning to get just a little peeved. Why do women have to be like that? 'I don't know,' I said. 'Nothing much happened.'

She relaxed a little. 'You're alright, Nick,' she said. 'It's me that's the arsehole as usual.'

'I don't think so, Sheila,' I told her. 'Anyway, it's purely academic. Stop beating yourself up about it.' I looked at my watch. That was purely academic too. It was time to leave, and if I had any sense never return. But when did I ever have any sense? 'I should go,' I said.

She nodded. 'Perhaps you should.'

'Can I see you again?'

'You've seen about all there is to see already.'

'You know what I mean.'

'Yeah. I know what you mean. Do you want to?'

'Of course.'

'I don't know.'

'I said you'd go weird.'

'Did you? What, weirder than I am already?' This time she smiled.

I nodded as I got out of bed, found my jeans, sweatshirt, socks and shoes and got dressed. She had lain back in bed and watched my every move. When I was ready I stood awkwardly by the bedside and said, 'Can I call you?'

She nodded. 'Number's on the phone,' she said.

'I'll be off then.'

Her expression softened and she reached out for me. 'Come here,' she said.

I sat on the edge of the bed and we kissed gently, and I felt the tip of her tongue again. 'Don't leave it too long,' she whispered as I put my face into her hair.

'I won't,' I replied and left, collecting her number and my milk on the way. I never did get to read that Sunday's paper.

Three

I WENT HOME, finally made that cup of tea and spent the rest of the day nursing my hangover and thinking about Sheila and what had and hadn't happened. Mostly the latter. The flat seemed even emptier than ever if that were possible.

I didn't know whether to get in touch again or not. I was in a quandary. I kept saying to myself 'Forget it', followed ten minutes later by 'Why not?' That went on for bloody hours.

But I wanted to and eventually 'Why not?' won the day as I knew it would and I called her that evening when I figured she'd be home from work. She picked up after the second ring. 'Hello,' she said.

'Hi,' I said. 'It's me, Nick.' I felt like some sort of dumb teenager asking a girl out on his first date. That's the sort of effect she had on me.

'Hello, Nick,' she said, but there wasn't much enthusiasm in her voice. 'How are you?'

I hate that. The disinterest when you phone up a woman to ask her out. I knew it had been a mistake to call but I persevered. Lack of sense, see. 'Still hungover a bit,' I replied.

'Me too. Work was murder. We drank a little yesterday.'

'We sure did.' There was an awkward silence. 'I wondered if I could see you,' I said.

'Not tonight, I'm tired.'

'I didn't mean tonight. Soon.'

'I don't know.'

'What's the matter?' I asked.

'Nothing. I'm . . . I'm embarrassed if you want to know. It all came back to me. I forced you to stay.'

'Hardly. I'm a big boy now. If I'd wanted to go I would've gone.'

'No. I made a big deal out of it. I'm sorry.'

'Look, Sheila. I wanted to stay. I really did. And I'm glad. Don't be sorry, please.'

'Good. It's just that I'm a bit freaked out around men these days. Johnny did that. You know.'

'I know,' I replied. 'You were far too good for him.'

'Don't say that, it's not true.'

'I think it is.'

'You're a nice bloke, Nick. Where were you seven years ago when I was young and stupid and I believed every word that Johnny said?'

'I was around.'

'But not around me.'

There was no answer to that. 'So can I see you?' I asked again. I was starting to sweat.

'If you're sure.'

'Sure I'm sure.'

'Then on your own head be it, but don't say I didn't warn you.'

'Cross my heart.' Maybe I should've listened.

'When then?' she asked.

'Tomorrow?'

'Sure. What do you want to do?'

'Have a drink. A meal. Talk.'

'Talk huh? That sounds positively dangerous.'

'We could always communicate by sign language.'

'Or smoke signals.'

'Sounds reasonable.'

'You're quite mad.'

'But never boring.'

'Don't make me laugh, Nick, I think I'll throw up.'

'Please don't. I'm still not feeling at my best, remember.'

'But you didn't have to sit in a stuffy office all day.'

'True.'

'So what did you do?'

'Sat at home.' I was going to add 'and thought about you', but didn't think it was appropriate.

'The upside of self-employment.'

'And earned nothing.'

'The downside of self-employment.'

We were getting on better than I thought we would. 'So tomorrow's OK?' I asked.

'Sounds fine to me. I get home from work about six. Call for me at seven?'

'I'll look forward to it.'

There was a pause and I heard her breathe and I imagined her breath on my neck. 'Me too,' she said finally. 'Yeah. Me too.'

Four

WHEN I WENT to collect her the next night I was all
booted and suited in a dark blue three-button
Hugo Boss with a white, tab collared shirt and skinny
knitted tie. Very mod, I thought as I admired myself
in the mirror before I left. And I was shaved and had
washed my hair this time. On the way I wondered if I was
a bit overdressed, but when she answered the door she'd
made some effort too, wearing the same furry jacket, but
this time over a little black dress and black nylons. 'You
look nice,' I said.

She wrinkled her nose. 'Don't,' she said.

'You know most women enjoy compliments.'

'I'm not most women,' she replied.

'You can say that again.'

She smiled and I went in close and kissed her on
the cheek, inhaling her perfume. 'And you smell nice
too,' I said.

'So do you. What's that?'

'Paco Rabane,' I said. 'I read that he believes that the
angels sent him down to earth to bring fragrance to the
people, which is kind of worrying.'

She shrugged. 'Whatever makes him happy.'

'And rich.' I said. 'What do you want to do?'

'You said something about a drink. But maybe not as
much as last time.'

'So you won't be compromised?'

'Something like that.'

'I'll never compromise you.'

'I believe you, Nick.'

Thousands wouldn't, I thought.

We walked down to the main road and went into the
boozer. Maybe it wasn't the most romantic place in the

world, but there was a small, quiet bar at the back and I
wanted to talk to Sheila alone.

It was as deserted as I'd hoped it would be and I
rousted some service whilst she snagged a table. 'Gin
and tonic?' I said.

She nodded in reply.

When I'd got her drink and a beer for myself I joined
her. We clinked glasses and I said, 'Here's to crime.'

'And passion,' she replied.

'I'll drink to that.'

So we did.

'What's the story then?' I asked when I'd lit us a pair
of cigarettes.

'You tell me.'

'Come on, Sheila,' I said. 'Don't mess about. Is this it?
A polite drink and then a peck on the cheek, a promise
to be friends, and a sigh of relief when we say goodnight,
and never see each other again.'

'What's the alternative?'

'I think you know that.'

'But do *you*?'

'Meaning?' I asked.

'Meaning you might be biting off more than you can
chew.'

'I've done that before.'

'Not with me.'

'And what's so special about you?'

'Things.'

'Is that right?' I was getting a bit pissed off with her.
It's usually me that's enigmatic.

'That's right,' she said.

'What kind of things?'

'Many and varied. It could never be plain sailing.'

'Do you think that's what I expect? Or for that matter
want?'

'I don't know what you want, Nick.'

'You, I think.'

'Just think. That's not good enough. You'd have to be sure.'

'And if I am?' I said.

'There could be trouble. I don't want to lead you up the garden path.'

'I rarely, if ever, get led anywhere I don't want to go,' I told her, which is arrant nonsense if ever I've heard any.

'It's your funeral.' Although it wasn't as it turned out, but then neither of us could possibly have known that at the time.

'I'll risk it,' I said.

'Then fasten your seat belt, it could be a bumpy ride,' she said, and we touched glasses and that was that.

Five

WE ATE CHINESE, and although I was excited as hell being with Sheila I managed not to spill any yellow bean sauce down my tie.

We did what people always do at that stage of a relationship. A lot of talking, a bit of footsie, a bit of touching hands and a few long silences. And even though Sheila had suggested putting a bit of a block on the booze intake we still managed to get through a couple of bottles of wine between us with the food, and two double Rémys each with the coffee. I could tell this was going to turn into one of those alcoholic love affairs if it turned into anything at all. But then what did I care?

We walked back to her place hand in hand, bumping hips all the way, with the almond and cherry blossom falling onto her hair and my shoulders like confetti at a wedding. I hold that memory now in my heart as I sit here waiting for the police to come.

As soon as we got inside I grabbed her as her flat door slammed behind us and I slid my hand up her skirt. 'You're eager,' she said.

'S'pose so,' I said between kisses. 'Do you mind?'

'I'm not exactly a damsel in distress crying out to be rescued.'

'And I'm not exactly a knight in shining armour coming to your aid.'

'A bit tarnished is it, the old armour?'

'You could say that.' And I kissed her again.

She pulled back. 'Listen, big boy,' she said. 'Let's take it easy here.'

'If you say so.'

'Drink?'

'I thought we were being a little more abstemious.'

'It helps me relax.'

'I can do that.' I held up my hands. 'With these magic fingers of mine.'

She laughed out loud. 'What am I doing here?' she said.

'What *are* you doing here?'

'Falling in love with an idiot.'

'What did you say?' I asked.

'I said that you were an idiot.'

'No. Before that.'

'Can't remember.'

'Something about falling in love.'

'You must have misheard.'

'I don't think so,' I said.

'Maybe it just slipped out.'

'OK. Have it your way. Got any more brandy?'

'I got a bottle in specially.'

'To get me drunk?'

'Maybe.'

'So you could have your evil way with me?'

'Maybe.'

'Well let's get to it.'

I went and chose some music whilst she broke out the brandy. I picked out a CD by Frank Sinatra. *Songs for Swingin' Lovers.* Just right for a romantic night in I thought. Better than the soundtrack for *Natural Born Killers* anyway. She came back with the bottle and two glasses. 'You old softy,' she said. 'You know what to do to get a girl's knickers off, don't you?'

'It's just one of my inborn talents.'

She sat next to me and poured out two large drinks. We clinked glasses and drank. She picked up her bag and fumbled inside it for her cigarettes. 'Do I get the feeling you're prevaricating here?' I asked as we lit up.

'I'm still not sure this is such a good idea,' she said as

she blew smoke. 'I told you I'm a little freaked out around men these days.'

'And I think I told you I wouldn't fuck you up.'

'Not on purpose maybe.'

'Not at all.'

'Easy to say.'

'There's only one way to find out.'

'I know. That's what I'm afraid of.'

'What?' I asked.

'Finding out. Finding out you're just like all the rest.'

'There's no answer to that.'

'An enigma,' she said.

'Which is what you are.'

'I never promised it would be easy.'

'I know that. You're just not giving me much of a chance.'

'Poor baby,' she said.

'It's just that we're doing a lot of assuming here.'

'Assuming what?'

'That this has got somewhere to go.'

'Assuming the assumptions,' she said.

'And given the given,' I added.

'Of course. Always given the given.'

'I think this is where we reach a fork in the road.'

'That old fork in that old road,' she mused. 'It always seems to come down to that old fork in that old road.'

'Doesn't it just.'

'Every time.'

'So which direction do we take?' I asked.

'Nick. I honestly don't know.'

'Listen, if you want me to go . . .'

'No I don't. I didn't want you to go on Sunday and I don't want you to go now. Just give me a little time.'

'We've got all the time in the world.'

She was suddenly serious. 'No, Nick. I don't think we do.'

'Meaning?'

'Meaning nothing. I'm talking bollocks.' She stubbed out her cigarette. 'Why don't you kiss me.'

So I did.

Later, when we were both naked in her bedroom in the semi dark with just stripes of light coming through the curtains from the street lights outside, I lay with my head on her stomach. It was white and smooth and I slid my tongue into her belly button.

'That tickles,' she said.

'Tastes good though.' I said, and looked up at her. Her green eyes shone like a cat's in the gloom. Her eye make-up had been rubbed off and she looked about twelve years old.

I told her so and she giggled. 'I am,' she said. 'That's my secret. Twelve going on twenty nine.'

'And you smell like heaven.'

'I didn't think you'd be like this.'

'What?'

'So sweet. You've got a bad reputation.'

'Have I?'

'Yes. I thought you'd be more like Johnny. He didn't go in for foreplay a lot. A wham-bam-thank-you-ma'am kind of guy.'

'And I'm not.'

'No you're not. For instance you didn't force yourself on me the other night. Johnny would've loved to have an unconscious woman to screw. Then he could've just rolled over afterwards and gone to sleep.'

'I couldn't do that.'

'I know. Or at least I know now. But I've heard stories about you.'

'Sheila,' I said, and pulled myself up close to her. 'What I do outside in the world is one thing. Sometimes it's got pretty rough I agree. But that's what I do. In here with you it's another thing altogether. It's private, between you and me. And it's real. It's what matters. I'm already beginning to think it's the only thing that does matter.'

'I feel the same way baby,' she said, and kissed me.
'Good,' I said into her mouth.
'So make love to me.'
And I did that too.

Six

WE LAY TOGETHER shoulder to shoulder afterwards, drinking the remains of the brandy we'd brought with us into the bedroom and smoking. 'You're good,' she said.

'I bet you say that to all the boys.'

She dug me in my ribs with her elbow. Hard. Hard enough to hurt. 'I do not,' she said.

I could tell I'd boobed. 'Joke,' I explained.

'I don't like jokes like that.'

'Sorry.'

After a moment she rubbed the spot where she'd hit me. 'See,' she said. 'There I go being daft again.'

'No. There I go being thoughtless again.'

She gave me a hug. 'No you're not,' she said. 'You're good.'

'You already said that.'

'I meant in lots of ways, not just in bed.'

I was a bit more careful with the reply this time. 'You're not bad yourself,' I said. 'In lots of ways too.'

'A little out of practice between the sheets maybe.'

'Me too.'

'I doubt that.'

'Listen, I know I have this not undeserved reputation of being a bit of a ladykiller, but believe me Sheila, for a long time now I've been cuddling my pillow at night.'

'Oh, shame.'

'I agree. But I was waiting for Miss Right to come along.'

'My name's Madden.'

'You know what I mean.'

'Course I do. So maybe we should practise some more then.'

'I think we should practise on a regular basis.'

'Like how often?'

'At least twice a day until we get it right.'

'But I'm a perfectionist,' she said.

'So it might take a while.'

'So maybe more than twice a day.'

'Maybe.'

'Still might take a while.'

'That's a possibility.'

'A long while.'

'There's no knowing how long,' I said.

'Years,' she suggested.

'Decades,' I countered. If only I'd known then what I know now, that we had so little time, that it could have been counted in days rather than years.

'Centuries.' She was laughing by then.

'Sounds rough to me.'

'A living hell,' she said.

'But we'll have to persevere.'

'Perseverance is a virtue.'

'And you're a very virtuous woman.'

'It's nice of you to point that out.'

'I try to please.'

'You succeed. Or at least you've succeeded so far. Just don't get lazy.'

'Can't I just lie back and enjoy it?'

'That's my job. Your job is to work very hard at pleasing me.'

'OK,' I said. 'I'll remember that.'

'You'd better.'

'I promise.'

'I love you, Nick.' Her words could almost have been written in multi-coloured neon on the darkness of the wall opposite, so brightly did they shine.

'Did I mishear again?' I asked after a moment. One of those moments that was as fragile as a soap bubble.

'No. Not this time.'

'Heavy duty.'

'Did I say the wrong thing?' she asked.

'Not at all.'

'Well?'

'Well what?'

'Don't do this to me, Nick.'

'What?' I asked innocently.

'You know.'

I laughed and grabbed her and kissed her hard. 'Sorry, sweetheart, I just wanted to get you mad.'

'You're doing it.'

'You're beautiful when you're mad.'

'It's dark, you can't see.'

'Well you're beautiful when you're not mad so I just assumed . . .'

'Oh Nick.'

'And I love you too.'

'Do you mean it?'

'Of course.'

'There's no "of course" about it.'

'Trust me.'

'I do. That's one of the reasons I said it to you.'

'I love you Sheila. Scout's honour.'

'You were never a boy scout.'

'Sure I was. Eighteenth Streatham, I was leader of the Eagle patrol.'

'Did you wear shorts?'

'Yep.'

'With your bony knees?'

'My knees are OK.'

She burst into peals of laughter and it made me feel good to hear her. 'Jesus, but you're priceless,' she said.

Seven

WE SPENT EVERY night that week together. We ate, drank, made love, laughed and talked. Man, how we talked. Or at least she did. I mostly listened. Mostly in the dark in bed after lovemaking with sometimes just the spark of the coals from our cigarettes as illumination.

She told me about her life. Her mother and father who were both dead, and her younger sister who she didn't see since she'd taken up with Johnny Tufnell. She didn't explain why, but I could guess. I presumed that little sister had seen through him like the rest of us and told Sheila some home truths on the subject, which I imagine didn't go down too well. In fact, knowing Sheila as I did by then I was sure they didn't, even if she knew them to be spot on. And she told me about Johnny himself. How they'd met and how she'd fallen for his oily charms and how she'd stayed with him for nearly seven years of ritual beating and humiliation. Why she'd stayed she didn't know. But as I lay there next to her I got to really hate him for what he'd done to her, but I said little about it. I sensed that if I'd promised retribution she would have loved me less. And I didn't want that. I wanted her to love me more. Like I loved her more every single second I was with her. And besides, Tufnell was history. She hadn't heard of him for months. He was gone.

Gone, but not forgotten.

On Saturday morning when she didn't have to work, I got up quietly, left her in bed and went down to the shops to get the makings of breakfast, Sheila's idea of domestic and cooking arrangements being a little sparse. I bought eggs, bacon, tomatoes, mushrooms, a can of beans, orange juice, bread and milk. Plus the papers of course. I went back, checked on her still comatose form and started cooking. The smell of grilling bacon must have roused her because she came into the kitchen in her dressing gown, one shapely breast almost exposed, and said, 'What's all this?'

'I fancied cooking.'

'I'm not used to being waited on.'

'Get used to it. I could've run a kitchen. Maybe I did in another life.'

She jumped up and kissed me. 'Nick. I've always wanted a little wife. Looks like I've got one.'

'Have fun' I said. 'Take the piss as much as you like. Just remember you'll pay later.'

'Is that a threat or a promise?'

'You work it out.'

'Have I told you lately that I love you?' she asked after she'd tasted the beans and left a little smudge of juice on her chin.

'Good title for a song,' I replied, catching the sauce with my thumb then licking it off. 'And no. Not since about three this morning.'

'I was asleep at three this morning.'

'No you weren't. And nor were the neighbours the way you were screaming out my name.'

'Must've been on TV.'

'Sure, honey,' I said, flipping two eggs on to plates. 'That's your story. I'd stick to it if I was you.'

'You're beautiful,' she said, as I laid out the rest of the breakfast and poured coffee into two mugs.

'I always told you that. You just realised?'

'Fool.'

We sat in the kitchen and ate and read the papers I'd bought, then we went into the living room and she said, 'What are we going to do today?'

'Dunno. What do you fancy doing?'

'Dunno,' she mimicked, 'but it's a nice day. Too nice to spend it in bed.'

'Tired of me already, is that it?' I asked. 'Or am I just wearing you out?'

'Neither. But I thought we could do something together.'

'Seems to me we've been doing things together for the last few days.'

She blushed. I loved that about her, that she could still blush when I said something like that. 'Nick, you're embarrassing me,' she said. 'And I'll never be able to look at the neighbours again.'

'They'll get over it,' I said. It occurred to me that they must've heard plenty when Tufnell had been knocking her about, but thought it politic not to mention that.

'So what are we going to do today?' she asked after a minute.

'Want to go to the seaside?'

'Are you kidding?' She was like a little child and my heart melted.

'No kidding. Let's go to Brighton.'

Eight

ONCE WE'D DECIDED there was no stopping her, especially when I told her we'd stay over. 'God, I need to pack,' she said. 'I haven't got a thing to wear.'

'We're only going for one night,' I said. 'And last time I looked you had a wardrobe full of things to wear.'

'Fat lot you know,' she told me in that way women have as if they're talking to a simpleton. 'Where are we going to stay?'

'Dunno,' I replied.

'I'll need a sea view and a balcony.'

'Need? You don't need much do you? I expect The Grand and The Metropole are booked up.'

'Too expensive for you, handsome? Don't worry, I'll pay my way,' she said, wrinkling her nose like I was a bad smell.

'You know that's not what I mean. And forget about paying. I invited you. Remember?'

'You going to treat me?'

'Sure.'

'How are we getting there?'

'We'll drive. I'll get my car. You get ready and I'll pick you up in half an hour.'

She didn't bother to reply, just went to her wardrobe and started sorting clothes.

I went home, showered, shaved, changed clothes, threw a clean shirt, underwear, socks and shaving gear into a bag and went round to the lock-up garage that had come vacant on the next street where I'd been keeping my car. That year I was driving a 1969 Ford Mustang coupé. It was a brutal motor, 5.7 litre engine, automatic gearbox, power steering, power discs all round, cherry bombs on the exhaust so that the car sounded like Concorde landing, a front spoiler, mag wheels and fat tyres under a lowered suspension and full race interior. It took a bit of starting and played up until it was warm, but then it went like shit off a shovel. Inside the cockpit it was all original with an AM radio and eight track stereo. Remember them? You can get the cartridges for fifty pence if you know what junk shops to look in. I do. Unfortunately one of the downsides is that you're not spoiled for choice on the titles available. Lots of Pink Floyd and Genesis I'm afraid, but occasionally a gem will show up. Another downside is the fact that they're roughly the size of a paperback book and are notoriously unreliable. The upside is that you're unlikely to have your car stereo nicked.

I climbed in the motor, pumped the accelerator and turned the key. It started on the third turn, stalled as I put it into gear, then started when I twisted the key again. I reversed out into the street, left the engine running whilst I shut the garage door and locked it, and drove round to Sheila's. She'd never seen the car and her eyes widened when she came out of her front door carrying a suitcase big enough for a world cruise. 'Is this yours?'

'Yes.'

'It's gorgeous.'

'Check the owner.'

She didn't bother to reply as she climbed into the front bucket seat which I'd emptied of eight track cartridges, and after I'd stowed her luggage I helped her with the seat belt, making sure I touched her breasts as I did so.

'Have you taken many women out in this?' she demanded. I shook my head.

'Good. You were too handy when you belted me up.'

'All part of the service ma'am.'

'Sure.'

It took us just about an hour and a half to get to Brighton, and I showed off all the way, screeching the tyres and over-revving the engine until the cherry bombs howled.

'You're a flash fucker,' she said when we were driving sedately down the front.

'My middle initials are F. F.' I said.

I didn't bother with the really posh hotels, they're always full, but just down the road on the way to Hove we found exactly what she wanted. A hotel with one double room vacant, complete with a sea view and balcony just like the lady ordered. The balcony wasn't all that big, but the view was great and she was as happy as a pig in shit.

It's funny that. I've always found that laid back people are dead hard to please. Always moaning. But hard to please people are easy. Just give them exactly what they want and they roll over and let you tickle their tummies. Sheila did anyway.

And when I'd tickled her tummy enough we got dressed and went out to eat.

She'd brought enough clothes for a month and finally settled on a grey, forties style two piece suit with a real tight skirt.

When she was dressed she craned round to look at her back view in the mirror and asked the same question that every woman I've ever known asks sooner or later.

'Is my butt too big?'

Every woman, I swear. Eventually they get round to it. Is my butt too big? Or my backside, or bum, or arse, or ass if they're American, or posterior, or *derrière*, or rear, or fanny or any damned alternative word they can think of. I've heard that question a thousand times put a thousand different ways, so much so that it's become a joke. And yet they still do it. And I always answer it the same way. Just like I did when she asked me. 'It's perfect,' I said. 'A dream. A rhapsody. The cutest one I've ever seen.'

'You're so insincere.'

'Shallow even.'

'But you don't have to stop,'

'Don't tell me you're beginning to like compliments?'
I asked.

She held up her forefinger and thumb till they almost
touched. 'A bit,' she replied.

'I knew I'd win in the end.'

'Don't be so smug, shut up and take me out to eat.'

So I did.

Nine

THE EVENING WAS warm and we went to this buzzing Italian restaurant I know at the top of The Lanes. We strolled there hand in hand through the crowds of tourists, but we might just as well have been the only two people in Brighton that evening for all the notice we took of them.

The restaurant was still there, and already packed out, but we managed to get a table under the stairs where it was relatively quiet. When we were seated comfortably with the ever present bottle of red and two cigarettes going, Sheila said, 'Have you brought lots of women down here for a dirty weekend?'

'Is that what it is?' I asked wide eyed. 'Goody.'

'Answer the damned question.'

I thought for a minute, hiding behind my glass. I thought about other women, other times and places. 'One or two,' I said.

'There's a lot I don't know about you, Nick.'

'There's a lot a lot of people don't know.'

'You'll have to tell me.'

'Sometime,' I said.

'Soon.'

'I wouldn't want to bore you.'

'I thought you said you never were.'

'Maybe I was exaggerating.'

'I don't think so.'

'Really?'

'You've never bored me.'

'So far. There's lots of time.'

'I suppose so. Do I bore you?'

I pretended to think. Dangerous territory again. 'Of course not, my sweet,' I replied.

'Don't take the piss.'

'*Moi*?'

'Yes you. Come on tell me, have I?'

'Not for one minute. Honest.'

She reached over and touched my hand. 'I'm so glad we met that day and that you came back after I was so strange about it. A lot of men wouldn't have.'

'I'm not a lot of men.'

'You can say that again.'

I put down my cigarette and covered her hand that was touching mine. 'I love you Sheila,' I said.

'Truly.'

'Cross my heart and hope to die.'

She pulled her hand away quickly. 'Don't say that.'

'What's the matter?'

She shook off the question with a shrug. 'Nothing. It's just me. Come on, we're supposed to be having a good time. Let's choose.' And she picked up the menu, opened it and hid her face away from me.

I didn't think anything much about it then. I was too happy. Later I did.

We ate a lot, got half pissed and went back to the hotel holding hands again and looking in the windows of the antique shops in The Lanes before hopping a cab for the short run down to the front. We were both eager to be alone and left the lights in the room off, the balcony curtains wide and the french doors open so that we could hear the traffic and the people on the front below us and the sea beating on the pebbles of the beach beyond it.

We made love, then raided the mini bar and took our booty to bed. Sitting up drinking and smoking we could see the lights of the ships on the black horizon and the stars above them.

That night she let me talk. I told her about my wives and what had become of them. My daughters, and what had become of them. One alive and living in Scotland, the other curled up next to her mother in the black earth of

Greenwich. I told her about lots of things, some I'd never mentioned to a living soul before.

'You've had a rough time,' she said.

'Not as bad as some I could mention. I'm still here. Still standing. Barely. At least I'm alive.'

'I think you're very brave.'

'Bravery is a relative concept. Sometimes I think it's just being so scared and frightened you don't dare show it.'

'You've got friends though. People who've stuck by you.'

'You should never count on other people, I've found. They always let you down sooner or later. The cock crows three times and they fuck you over.'

'Including me?'

'I hope not.'

'I trust you and I hope you trust me. I won't let you down, Nick.'

I could see her green eyes shining in the dark again and I put one finger over her beautiful lips. 'Don't say that,' I said. 'You could live to regret it.'

She shook her head and kissed my finger and I forgot the remark in the heat of her body.

The next day we had a late breakfast and the Sunday papers delivered to the room and lounged around until checking out time, when we collected the car from the NCP where I'd left it and drove back to London, diverting for lunch in a country pub near Pease Pottage.

We got back to London around five and I dumped the car and we walked back round to her place where I spent the night again.

The next morning I watched her get ready for work. Before she left she said, 'Will you do me a big favour?'

'Sure. Just name it.'

'I have an envelope. I want you to keep it for me.'

'Why?'

'I just don't want it here. It's personal papers and things.

Have you got somewhere you could keep it safe for me?
Very safe.'
    'Sounds mysterious.'
    'No. It's just bits. But I don't want it here.'
    'Something to do with Johnny?'
    'No. Yes. Not really. Will you keep it for me?'
    'Course.'
    She went to the wardrobe and hunted round on one of
the shelves before producing a big, legal sized Jiffy bag
secured with one of those metal clips that goes through a
thin washer. It looked bulky and heavy and she put it next
to me on the bed. I hefted it in one hand. It was heavy. 'All
your worldly goods?' I asked jokingly.
    'If you like. Take it with you. I don't want it here. If
I need anything out of it I'll ask. Just put it somewhere
and forget about it and go on with your life. Don't tell me
where.'
    'I take it it's private.'
    'Very.'
    'But you haven't sealed it.'
    'I told you I trusted you. I know you won't look inside
if I ask you not to.'
    'Naturally.'
    'There. See what I mean. Now are we going out tonight?'
    'Of course. I couldn't go a day without seeing you.'
    'Flatterer.'
    'Not at all.'
    She kissed me and left, and in time I got up, got dressed,
made the bed, had a cup of coffee and headed home taking
the envelope with me. I didn't look inside. She was right.
She could trust me. Instead, I put it untouched into my
secret place underneath the roof of my flat where I keep the
two guns I still have as a souvenir of old times. Of course I
was tempted to open the envelope and look at its contents,
who wouldn't be? And don't forget my job is poking my
nose into other people's business. But Sheila had put her
faith in me and I wanted to prove that she was right to

do so. If I had opened it things would have worked out a whole lot differently, but we've all got 20/20 hindsight so I just tossed it up into the space under the slates with the seal unbroken.

Then I did what she said. I forgot all about it and got on with my life.

Ten

M Y DAUGHTER JUDITH called me from Scotland that evening.

'Hi, Dad,' she said.

'Hi, darling.'

'How's it going?'

'Not bad. You?'

'Not bad.'

Monosyllabic. She was seventeen then, and I suppose that's how seventeen-year-old girls talk to their estranged fathers. I hadn't seen her for months, so that's how I felt – estranged. 'How's school?' I asked after a second's pause.

'Not bad.'

'Good,' I said. She was coming to the end of her school career. Next stop university, her being no slouch with the books.

There was another pause, then she said, 'Dad, I've got something to tell you.'

'What?'

'I've met someone.'

Oh dear, I thought, she's pregnant, run away to Gretna Green. Married. Exit university, enter dirty nappies and a council flat in Leith. 'Who?' I asked with just the slightest catch in my voice.

'Don't sound like that.'

'Like what?'

'Like you've just swallowed a pill.'

'Sorry. Who?'

'A bloke.'

'I gathered that.'

'It doesn't always follow. Not these days.'

'Fair enough. I stand corrected. But it is a bloke.'

'Yes.'

'When?'

'When what?'

'When did you meet?'

'A few weeks ago.'

'Yeah?' My mouth was dry. Her first boyfriend. A day I'd always dreaded as she grew up and left me. But if it was only a few weeks then maybe my worst fears were unfounded.

'Yeah.'

'Is it serious?' I asked.

'Could be.'

I wasn't going to ask if she was sleeping with him. I refused to do that. 'It either is or it isn't,' I said, and almost bit off my tongue.

'Not necessarily.'

So she wasn't sleeping with him. Thank God for that. 'What's his name?' I said.

'Jerry, with a "J".'

'Is he Scottish?'

'Does it matter?'

'No. Just tell me he hasn't got red hair.'

'Oh, Dad, you are funny. He's not Scottish as a matter of fact, and he hasn't got red hair so there.'

'Where's he from?'

'London. He's up here at Uni.'

'How old is he?'

'Nineteen.'

'A good age,' I said, for the sake of something better.

'We're coming down for a visit.'

'To London?'

'Yes.'

'When?'

'Next weekend. He's driving.'

'What car's he got?' Stupid question and we both knew it.

'Oh, Dad. It's a Ford Escort as if it really matters.'

'Fair enough.'

'He wants to meet you, and I'm going to meet his mum and dad.'

'It is serious then.'

'No. It's just a break. I wanted to see you too. I haven't seen you for ages.'

'Sorry.'

'So is it alright?'

'Of course. Where will you stay?'

'At his. His folks have got some massive place in Highgate.'

'Blimey. They must be loaded.'

'I don't know. His father's something in the city.'

'Makes me look pretty downmarket.'

'Don't be silly. Anyway, we can go out for dinner.'

'Sounds good,' I said, and added, 'I'm seeing someone too.' I didn't want her to think I was a lonely loser with a one-room flat in Tulse Hill compared to something in the city and his wife with a mansion in Highgate.

'Are you?'

'Yes.'

'Good. I hate it when you're on your own.'

I didn't bother to let her in on the secret that we're all on our own. 'Thanks.'

'Is it serious?' she asked in a parody of my question.

'I think so.'

'What's her name?'

'Sheila.'

'What does she do?'

'She's a legal secretary.'

'Useful in your line of work.'

'He's a pretty dodgy brief.'

'I wouldn't expect anything else.'

'Thank you so much.'

'Just kidding. Why don't we make up a foursome?'

'What a good idea,' I said. But it wasn't, and it wasn't any of our faults.

'Does he eat normal food, your Jerry?' I asked.

'Course he does. And he walks upright and his hands hardly drag on the floor at all.'

'You know what I mean. He's not a veggie or anything.'

'I know what you mean, Dad. And no he's not a veggie, or an eco-warrior or anything like that. He's just a normal bloke. And he wants to see south London,' she said.

'Why?'

'Because I've told him so much about it.'

'Hasn't he ever been? You don't need a passport you know, whatever people say.'

'As a matter of fact I don't think he has. Just passed through. You know what people from north London are like.'

I certainly did. 'I certainly do,' I said.

'So can we? Visit the flesh pots of West Norwood I mean?'

'I suppose.'

'And you'll bring Sheila.'

'Yeah.'

'Right. Saturday night.'

'Whatever you say.'

'Great. I'd better go. Love you, Dad.'

'Love you, darling.'

And we both hung up.

Eleven

I TOLD SHEILA about the call the next day. 'You don't mind do you?' I asked.

'Mind what?'

'Coming along. Making up a foursome, as Judith so neatly put it.'

'No,' she replied. 'If you don't.'

'Not in the least,' I said. 'I'd like you two to meet.'

'Get her approval.'

'I think it's a bit late for all that, don't you?'

'If you say so.'

'And besides, I think she's just relieved I've got someone. That I don't just sit at home at night dribbling my chocolate biscuits and Ovaltine down my pyjama jacket.'

'Poor old you.'

'And it's her first proper boyfriend. It might be better to have someone else there.'

'As a referee?'

'If you like.'

'To stop you tearing his throat out.'

'Is it that obvious?'

'It wouldn't be more obvious if you were armed with a trident and a net.'

'Blimey. It's not that I'm jealous . . .'

'Not much.'

'She's all I've got left,' I said. 'Of a family,' I added.

'I'm glad you said that.'

'And she's so young.'

'Old enough to get married.'

'Don't say that.'

'Nick. From what you've told me she's a sensible girl.'

'With no mother.'

'That's hardly your fault.'

'Some people wouldn't see it that way.'
'Stop feeling sorry for yourself.'
'OK.'
And we left it at that.

Twelve

O F COURSE THE evening was a disaster like I said, but it wasn't my fault for once. Unless the choice of venue had anything to do with it, which was my choice. Sheila and I had discovered a little Thai restaurant just off Streatham High Road. It didn't look like much from the outside, more like a greasy spoon than anything else, but it was licensed and the food was great. It was run by a mom and pop team assisted by an apparently inexhaustible supply of young sons and daughters, nephews and nieces. It was tiny, the tables were formica topped and the cutlery didn't match. In a way I suppose I was showing off to Jerry with a 'J', Highgate's finest. 'You want to slum it down south London way,' I suppose I was saying, 'then walk this way.'

And strangely enough, in a way it mirrored all that was to happen later that summer although at the time I had no way of knowing.

First of all the weather. It was pouring with rain that Saturday. It had poured all day and the forecast on the TV said that there was no sign of it stopping before morning.

Sheila came to my place and Judith and Jerry were going to pick us up in his car. According to the follow up call I'd had from my daughter he didn't drink much. In a way that was reassuring, but in another it wasn't. Humphrey Bogart said he never trusted a man who didn't drink and smoke. But then the kid was only nineteen so there was plenty of time, and besides, things were different when Humphrey was around.

Then they were late and I had visions of a pile up on the Walworth Road, but Judith called on his mobile. The Escort had water in its carbs and they'd had to call the AA.

Judith was all flustered when they arrived and showed it, and he was too, but tried to stay cool. I tried to stay cool too as we exchanged introductions. In fact he was quite a personable young man wearing chinos, a rugby shirt and leather jacket. Hair long, but not noticeably so, and a firm handshake. Judith looked beautiful in a plain grey dress and Sheila had chosen basic black with just a little make-up and she looked beautiful too. Me. I was in faded jeans, a blue button down Oxford cotton shirt and my only jacket: a grey Boss single breasted with side vents. I felt like a lecturer at a provincial polytechnic. All I needed was black horn rims and I'd've been perfect for the Michael Caine part in *Educating Rita*.

I offered drinks. I needed one but had been most abstemious all afternoon. The last thing I wanted to do when they turned up was to be pissed. Judith and Jerry had Coke, Sheila went for a gin and tonic and I had a beer. All very civilised.

'Well I suppose we'd better make a move,' I said when the glasses were empty.

'Have you booked, Dad?' asked Judith.

'You don't book where we're going,' I said mysteriously.

'Little Chef?' said Judith.

'Not quite.'

It was still pouring out so I took a big golf umbrella when we went to the car, and sheltered the women. Blimey, but it's strange thinking of Judith as a woman rather than a little girl. But by the look of her that evening she was all woman and make no mistake.

It was a short ride inside the misted up Escort to the High Road, but of course we had to park a quarter of a mile from the restaurant and I was glad of the brolly as we all four tried to huddle beneath it during the walk there from the motor.

The place was three-quarters full when we arrived and as we went inside we had to negotiate a large puddle of rainwater that had collected under the front door where it failed to reach the floor by about half an inch. We grabbed the last table for four just inside the small front window and the momma took my umbrella out to the back. She looked a little flustered and there was no sign of papa.

'Where is he?' I asked as she took our order for the starters, more Cokes and a bottle of white wine for Sheila and me.

'Downstairs,' she said with a grimace. 'He's not well.'

'What's the matter?' I asked. 'Nothing serious I hope.'

'Too much rain,' she said enigmatically, and left us.

Judith made a quizzical face at me and I shrugged in return.

I offered cigarettes but there were no takers so I desisted too. One of the daughters, or maybe it was a niece, brought prawn crackers, the soft drinks and the wine.

'Interesting place,' said Jerry when everyone had a full glass, but what he meant was 'what a dump'.

I suddenly realised I'd made a mistake bringing us there, as the puddle inside the door grew larger as the rain came down harder.

'Homely,' I said.

'It's one of our favourites,' said Sheila defensively. 'The food's great.'

'Dad always did have eclectic taste in restaurants,' said Judith. I saw that she was getting the vibe from Jerry too. Heaven forbid she should turn into a little snob like he appeared to be.

The prawn crackers vanished post haste and Jerry made an approving face, which was something, and the rain coursed down the window, so that passing cars, headlights on, shimmied across the surface of the glass like neon ghosts.

We made small talk about Scotland and Judith's choice of universities, which I hoped was going to be down south close to London, but that she hinted might be nearer Jerry in Aberdeen. How they met at a student party, which gave

ALL THE EMPTY PLACES

me nightmares of necking tabs of 'E', getting loved up and going at each other hammer and tongs. But as Judith had had some small experience of that some years before, I didn't mention it, and then the starters came. It had taken an inordinately long time for them to arrive and the first bottle of wine was no more than a memory so I ordered more, although I caught a dirty look from Sheila as I did so, and I realised I'd drunk most of the first all by myself.

We dug into a selection of Thai spring rolls, ribs cooked in the speciality honey sauce, butterfly prawns and miniature pork dim sum.

'These are delicious,' said Jerry. 'I must say this place is much better than it looks.'

You little prat, I thought.

Whilst we were eating, from beneath us where the kitchens were situated I could hear the sound of altercation.

'What's going on?' asked Judith.

'Don't ask me,' I replied, through a mouthful of prawn. 'Sounds like the chef's getting a bit excited.'

The sounds of argument got louder and I recognised the voice of the pop screaming in English.

'Why don't you go and see?' asked Sheila.

'No,' I said. 'I think their kitchen is sacrosanct, and besides there's too many sharp objects down there.'

I'd meant it as a joke but suddenly the daughter or niece or whatever appeared in the doorway, white as a sheet, and started yelling in what I assumed to be Thai.

'There's something wrong, Dad,' said Judith, with a worried look on her face that recalled her mother so exactly that it hurt.

The girl came running to our table. 'Please help me,' she begged. 'Father. Downstairs.'

As I was standing, mom came through the door also and I saw that the front of her apron was bloodstained, and the joke about sharp edges suddenly wasn't so funny.

'Quick,' she cried. 'Call the police someone, and an ambulance.'

Jerry took out his mobile and dialled three nines and I went to momma and said, 'What's happening?'

She replied in her native tongue. 'I don't understand,' I said, and went to the door that opened onto the stairs that led down to the basement. Poppa was coming up, his shirt front and hands also bloody from cuts in his fingers and palms that literally squirted blood.

'Jesus,' I said as he collapsed on the stairs. I went to him and when I got up close I could smell whisky so strongly that he might have been bathing in the stuff. So much for 'too much rain'.

'Leave him,' said a woman's voice from behind me. 'I'm a doctor.'

A young woman from another party of four joined me and knelt beside the old man, who suddenly voided his bowels and the rich smell of faeces joined the stink of blood and whisky in a sickening stew.

I stepped over the old man and gingerly went downstairs to where the chef was standing in the kitchen, amidst pots and pans that were boiling over on the two industrial sized stoves against the far wall, waving a bloodstained knife in his right hand. To one side there was a cutting block upon which were strewn playing cards and a lot of cash. 'Get away,' he hissed, in heavily accented English.

Now how the hell did I get into this situation? I thought. When all I wanted was chicken noodles and duck in fruity sauce. 'Don't do anything daft,' I said, for the want of anything better.

'I'll kill you.'

'Why?'

'You and that old man want to cheat me out of my money.'

The wages of sin, I thought, looking at the blood-spotted cash on the board. 'No mate,' I said. 'We just want to get him to hospital and for you to put the knife down.'

He waved it in my direction and from above I heard the

howl of sirens and heavy footsteps on the ceiling over my head. Reinforcements. Thank Christ for that.

'Give it up, mate, the police are here,' I said gently.

'Police. I spit on your stinking police.' And he did, if not on the coppers at least on the floor in front of me. There were more footsteps, this time on the stairs, and I saw a blue uniform out of the corner of my eye.

'Don't make life difficult,' I continued, waving the copper back with one hand. 'The old man'll be alright. It's just a few cuts. Give me the knife and you can save the dumplings.'

He looked at the food boiling over on the stove and I stepped forward. Bad mistake. He saw me coming and lunged with his knife hand so that the tip of the blade caught the sleeve of my jacket. I let him come, pulled him forward by his right arm and put on an arm lock, twisted viciously and the knife hit the deck point downward, quivering in the wood. 'Hey,' he yelled. 'That hurts.'

'Tough.'

The cop came in and I held the chef as he put on the cuffs. 'That was rather silly, sir,' said the constable.

'I know. Heat of the moment.'

'We'll need a statement. Are you hurt?' He indicated the tear in my sleeve with his eyes.

'No, mate,' I replied. 'My family's upstairs and they're probably freaking out. I'm not going to press charges. He didn't draw blood.' And with that I ran up the stairs, past the old man who was being looked after by paramedics, and back into the restaurant proper where Sheila, Judith and Jerry were standing, looking worried. Through the water on the window I could see blue lights from the emergency vehicles flashing outside.

'Come on, let's go,' I said.

'Your arm,' said Judith.'

'It's nothing. Didn't even break the skin. Now come on, the cops want to talk to me, but I don't want to talk to them.'

We opened the door and the rain was coming down like bullets. 'Shit,' I said, went back to the door leading to the stairs and saw my umbrella leaning against the wall where the old man was lying. 'Sorry,' I said to the ambulance crew, reached over and picked it up. 'But it's pissing down out there.'

Momma caught us as we were leaving, our order in her hand. 'You didn't pay,' she said.

'Next time, darling,' I said as I ushered Sheila, Jerry and Judith out.

Christ, I couldn't believe it. I took my life into my hands and she still wanted me to pay for the meal. And we hadn't even got to the *entrée*.

We walked fast back to Jerry's car and I saw that his hands were shaking as he drove us back to my place. I don't mind admitting mine were shaking too. 'Coming in for a nightcap?' I asked when he stopped the car outside my door.

'I don't think so,' he replied. 'I'd better get Judith back.'

'Don't worry, Jerry,' said my daughter. 'Things always happen when Dad's around.'

Sheila and I climbed out of the back of the car and Judith got out and gave me a hug. 'I think it was when you went back for the umbrella that did it,' she said. 'See you, Dad.'

Sheila and I stood under the umbrella and watched as the tail lights of the Escort vanished into the gloom. 'Another night to remember,' she said drily, even though the rain was still thudding down around us.

Thirteen

JUDITH PHONED ME on Sunday morning early. 'Sorry about last night,' I said. 'Bit of a cock up in the catering department.'

'Don't worry,' she said. 'Jerry was a bit freaked at first, but I heard him on the phone last night to his room mate in Aberdeen. It's all turning into a bit of a legend. You soaked in blood taking on a mad chef. Sort of *South Park*, if you know what I mean.'

I did but I wasn't sure I wanted to.

'I'm sure by the time we get back up it'll be half a dozen knife crazed killers,' she went on. 'You're quite a hero.'

'A legend in my own dinner time. I was stupid. I should've left it to the police. Ruined my best jacket too.'

'Never mind.'

'Not much point is there?'

'So what did you think of him?' she asked, changing the subject. 'Come on, tell the truth.'

I hesitated.

'Come on, Dad.'

'At first I thought he was a snobby little prat,' I replied, after a few seconds. 'But he handled himself well in the emergency. And you look like you get on, so I'll give him the benefit of the doubt.'

'Well that's something.'

'How about Sheila?' I asked.

'She's great,' my daughter said without hesitation. 'Far too good for you.'

'Thank you.'

'Only kidding. I mean it. I'm glad you've found some-one so nice. Hang on to her.'

'I intend to. So when are you going back up to Scot-land?'

'This afternoon. It's a long drive. We'll stop off some-where for the night.'

'Single rooms?'

'*Dad*' she said, with a warning in her voice.

'Alright, I won't ask.'

'There's a good boy.'

I felt like a hundred years old. 'Well make sure he drives carefully,' I said.

'I will.'

'Call me soon.'

'Of course.'

And that was that. I smiled as I put the phone down. 'A hero.' If only they knew.

Fourteen

NOW ALL THAT had happened in the spring time, which came early that year, at least for me. And all through the three or four months that followed I don't think Sheila and I spent more than a few hours apart. I know we saw each other almost every day and I certainly never got tired of her company. We watched movies on video, ate out a lot, got drunk and high, went to the country and seaside again for weekends, laughed so much that sometimes we cried. And we fell more and more in love.

But we were waltzing towards our doom like two dancers on the edge of a precipice that they cannot see, until one day in early August, the lip of the precipice crumbled and everything went into free fall.

It was a Saturday, and Sheila had had to work late the previous evening and I'd been doing one of my rare jobs so that we hadn't seen each other since I'd stayed over on the Thursday night and we'd parted on Friday morning. It was the longest we'd been apart since we'd got serious about each other.

It was a simple job, delivering a summons for an old client who couldn't catch the recipient of the summons at home. Whenever my client's man went round, whoever answered the door denied all knowledge. I phoned the bloke's number and got a woman on the line. I told her I was a rep for one of the companies punting digital TV and that the gentleman concerned had won a wide screen telly that was ready to receive every channel under the sun. All he had to do was to sign for it. She fell for it hook, line and sinker, admitted that she was the summonsee's, if that's a word, wife, and told me he'd be in that very evening at seven. Then I went to my local TV shop and gave the kid who ran it a tenner for an empty cardboard box that had

once held just such a television set. I stuffed a load of
old phone books into the box until it had some weight
and staggered up the bloke's garden path that evening
at seven-fifteen, having parked the Mustang out of sight.
I could actually see the curtains twitch as I made a big
production of fumbling with the latch on the front gate,
and the geezer opened the door with a big smile on his
clock and was only too pleased to confirm his identity. It
was the same as the name on the summons that I slapped
into his hand. I dropped the box and its contents, and
legged it before he decided to get physical, leaving him
with just a dream of unlimited episodes of the *Simpsons*
for the rest of the new millennium.

All in all an easy two ton plus expenses earned for
a couple of hours' work. I went home, collecting an
American with onions and garlic from Pizza Express on
the way, and slobbed out in front of my own, admittedly
narrow screen, television for the rest of the evening with
my dinner, a couple of cans of lager, and the new Lawrence
Block paperback for company.

Oh happy day. It was to be the last for a long time.

I got up early the next morning, sang in the shower, got
all spruced up and sauntered round to Sheila's all ready
to go out and spend the dosh I'd earned the previous
evening. By that time I had a key to her flat and she to
mine. We'd talked about moving in together permanently,
but that would've meant selling one of the properties and
it was just too much hassle. Besides, it was only a few
minutes walk between the flats and it gave us our own
room within the relationship.

But I didn't need the key. When I got there the house
door was open, which was unusual, but I imagined that
the downstairs tenant had just slipped out somewhere for
a minute. I went inside and left it on the jar behind me,
then walked up the two narrow flights to Sheila's flat.
That door was open too. Just an inch or so, but it was the
kind of inch I'd hated for a long time.

I stood outside for a minute and thought about other doors that had been left open for me and the horrible surprises that had often been behind them.

Then I shrugged off the thought. Hell. Maybe she'd lost her keys and had gone out for some cigarettes leaving the doors open behind her. But then she was always so conscious of what could happen in that lovely part of town to people who did stupid things like that.

So I just pushed the door open gently and stuck my head round the jamb. It had been bright outside, with the hot August sun bouncing off the windows of the houses and the metal of cars, and my eyes had not got properly adjusted to see clearly in the gloom of her hallway.

'Sheila,' I called as I blinked, then saw what at first I didn't believe. There were dark streaks on the wallpaper that I'd never seen before, and the black and white checkered floor covering was spotted with more of the same.

Dark spots the colour of dried blood.

I still didn't believe it. Like I was hallucinating or having a bad dream. But I knew I was doing neither.

Without touching the door with my fingers, I pushed it open all the way and silently stepped into the hall. Outside I could hear birds singing, children shouting and the sound of the bass bin in a motor going by outside. But inside the flat all was silent. The bathroom was on my right, door open, empty. The kitchen was next to that. Ditto. The living room door was opposite the kitchen and open maybe a foot. I peered round it. The place looked like it had been spun. Sheila wasn't the tidiest of women but I'd've bet a tenner she hadn't left all the drawers in her tiny sideboard pulled out. There were more spots of blood on the carpet. The bedroom door was to my left. It was firmly closed. I walked quietly across the carpet, avoiding the mess, and with a tissue from the open box that lay on the sofa I turned the handle and pushed. The door swung away from me gently. Inside it was quiet except for the buzzing of a fly or bluebottle, and I wrinkled my nose as I smelled the stink of blood. The bedroom curtains were drawn as usual and the room was very dark. But for all the darkness I could see her white body lying across the burgundy coloured duvet that we'd slept under so many times. The whiteness only interrupted twice by the twin bands of her usual black underwear.

She was very still. 'Sheila,' I whispered. There was still no sound in the room except for that damned fly. No sound of breathing or the heartbeat I'd heard against mine so many times.

I took the few steps to the bed that felt like a thousand miles. I leant over and tweaked the curtain to allow the sunshine in and I winced. In the light I could see the blood that puddled on the duvet and was almost the same colour as it was. And I saw the cuts and slashes on her hands and arms where she had defended herself against whoever had attacked her. And worse, I saw the other mouth that had been cut in her throat and had dribbled her life force onto the bed.

I felt for a pulse but there was none. I sat down next to her and looked into her open, green eyes that were already glazing over as she stared into eternity.

I held one of her hands and the blood was still sticky. I closed her eyes with my fingers and sat there in that room of death with her as the golden slice of sunlight moved across her body. I must have sat there for an hour or more, holding her hand, until more flies attracted by the scent of her blood began to settle and feed and I could sit there no more. I was cold sitting there. Cold and shivery, even on that hot August morning that I'll always remember until the day I die. All kinds of emotions passed through my mind as I sat there. Mostly a terrible sorrow about what had happened. But I never cried once. In fact my eyes were so dry that I could hardly blink.

I spoke to her of course, but what I said was just for the two of us and no one else will ever hear the words. She was in a state of grace by then, far removed from earthly things.

Eventually, when I could sit there no longer I went into the living room and tapped out three nines on the phone, just holding the receiver by the very tips of my fingers.

It wasn't because I was afraid of leaving my fingerprints that I didn't touch anything. Rather it was that I was afraid of disturbing any forensic left by whoever had killed her. I mean my prints were all over the place, and I was well known by the neighbours, and I suppose that if she had left any dirty knickers lying about my DNA would be all over them.

When the exchange answered I asked for police. I told them that there had been a murder.

Then before I went out into the fresh air to have a cigarette and wait for the coppers to arrive, I went back into the bedroom one more time. I didn't know if I'd be able to see her again after. I didn't know if I'd have the nerve.

And as I looked down at her for the last time I realised with certainty that there were some lines that once drawn and crossed could never be re-crossed.

That there were some words that once spoken could never be unspoken.

And more importantly that there were some deeds that once done could never be undone.

Then I said goodbye.

Fifteen

I WAS JUST finishing my cigarette when the first police presence arrived in the shape of a crime car with blue lights flashing but no screamer on. Maybe they thought the noise would wake the neighbours, or frighten away the bad guys. Bit late for that I thought.

I dropped the cigarette, ground it into the pavement with the sole of my shoe and walked to the kerb to meet them. This was going to be just dandy.

Inside the car were two beefy uniforms I'd never seen before, so alike they could've been twins. They got out and converged on me. Close up the only difference between them was that one's cheeks were dotted with acne scars. 'Did you dial nine nine nine, sir?' Acne Scars asked me politely.

'That's right.'

'What appears to be the problem?'

Problem. I ask you. The problem was that my life had just turned upside down. 'I told them on the phone,' I said. 'My girlfriend's been murdered.'

'You're sure of that, sir?'

What a fucking clown. 'No,' I replied as calmly as possible. 'She always lies around on a Saturday morning with her throat cut,' and I clenched my fists so tightly I could feel my nails cutting the skin of my palms.

'I see, sir.' But of course he didn't.

'And you are?' The other one asked, straightening his hat and ignoring my sarcasm.

'My name's Nick Sharman.'

Acne Scars started writing in his notebook.

'And her name?'

'Sheila. Sheila Madden.'

'And where is she?'

I pointed behind myself at the open door of the house. 'In there. Two flights up. The flat door's open. She's in the bedroom. That's through the living room.'

'OK, Ken,' said Acne Scars to his mate. 'You take a look. I'll see to Mr Sharman here and call in.'

Ken went down the path and into the house. I followed him with my eyes and noticed that the curtains in the houses around were starting to twitch. Acne Scars bent down into the car, keeping a careful eye on me, and whispered into the radio. I knew what he was doing. He was informing the CAD room to alert the troops. CID, SOCO, forensic, the ambulance service and the coroner's office. The lot. And then they'd do a PNC check on me. Should make interesting reading.

Ken came back out as Acne Scars finished. He looked a little pale and nodded to his mate. I lit another cigarette. I was glad he was pale. I wanted him to puke all over his shiny shoes.

'When did this happen?' asked Acne Scars.

'I don't know. I wasn't there. I guess a few hours before I found her. She was beginning to stiffen.' I couldn't believe I was talking like this. So calmly, when the world had just stopped turning.

'And when was that? When you found her I mean.'

'A bit ago. I don't know.'

'And when did you call in?'

'A few minutes before you arrived. You were very prompt. The operator will have the time.'

'But you didn't call in straight away? The minute you found her? Or an ambulance? Why was that?'

'She was dead. There was nothing anyone could do. I wanted to spend some time with her.'

They looked at each other then as if I was some kind of necrophiliac nutter, but I didn't care. Neither of them would know how it felt until God forbid it happened to one of them. As we were speaking a crowd began to gather and gawp, and a Panda car arrived, driven by a WPC. Acne Scars told her to get the crowd back and she did.

'The paramedics might've been able to do something,' Ken said, when Acne Scars got back to us.

'Ken,' I said. 'I hope you don't mind me calling you Ken, but I don't know your other name. I used to be in the Job. I've seen some dead bodies before. She was past any help in this world and I wanted a few minutes with her. I'm sorry if that offends your sense of what's correct under the circumstances, but that's what happened.'

'And that helped her killer get away.'

'Is that right? She'd been dead some time when I found her. He was hardly going to be sitting down to tea and toast in her kitchen. He was long gone.'

'In your opinion.' Maybe he was right, maybe he was wrong. It didn't matter. All that mattered was that she was dead. The rest could take care of itself.

'It was the only opinion that mattered at the time,' I said. 'I found her.'

There was really no answer to that and we all knew it.

Then an unmarked saloon arrived and stopped behind the Panda. Two more men got out. I didn't know them either. I'd been out of the Job a long time. One of the new arrivals was middle-aged, wearing a jacket that was too warm for the weather, over a suit, the other in a leather blouson and jeans. 'CID,' said Acne Scars, closing his notebook with a snap. 'I'll get on.' And he went into the car, rummaged round in the glove box and came out with a roll of blue and white tape to mark the perimeters of the crime scene.

Ken waited for the two CID officers to get to us and told them who I was. They pulled him aside and had a whispered conversation I couldn't hear. I could just imagine what was being said. 'We've got a right one here. You want to watch him. He probably did for her himself.'

After a minute Ken went back to his mate and the CID

men came back to me. The middle-aged man flashed his warrant and said, 'Detective Sergeant Blackford, Denmark Hill. This is DC Hawes. Mr Sharman is it?'

I nodded.

He didn't seem to know me either. That would soon change, but right then it was a blessing. 'What exactly has been happening here?' he asked.

I reiterated my story and the two plainclothes coppers left me in the capable hands of Ken whilst they went inside and had a gander.

By the time they came out more cars and vans and the ambulance had arrived with the technical teams, and the crowd had got bigger, and the day had got hotter, and I was running out of cigarettes.

'Mr Sharman,' said Blackford. 'I think we should continue this down at the station.'

'Are you arresting me?' I asked.

'No, sir,' said Hawes. 'Whatever made you think that? Just a few questions.'

'I think I need my solicitor,' I said as we walked to their car.

'Any particular reason?' asked Blackford mildly. 'You haven't done anything wrong have you, sir?'

'No,' I replied. 'I'd just feel more comfortable with him around.'

'Then you can call him from the station.'

'I don't have his home number. And it's Saturday.'

'Don't worry, Mr Sharman,' said Hawes as he opened the back door of their car so I could get in. 'I'm sure we can sort something out. And mind your head now, sir.'

At least he was still calling me sir.

Sixteen

WE ROLLED INTO Denmark Hill police station at just a few minutes before ten o'clock that interminable morning. It was a Victorian building, built like a Noddy house out of brick with a slate roof that gleamed dully in the sunshine. An old-fashioned blue lamp hung outside the front door, and there were even hanging baskets of flowers to soften the harsh lines of the place. But I knew that the windows were bulletproof glass, the front door had been strengthened with steel, and inside it would still smell of bad coffee and human misery like every other police station I'd ever been inside.

There had been no conversation on the short car ride there. Not between me and the coppers or the coppers between themselves. I sat in the back of the motor and looked out at all the people getting on with their lives, when as far as I was concerned they should've stopped. Should've covered their faces and mourned for Sheila. But to them she was nothing. A footnote in the evening news. Maybe a moment of *frisson*, a few words of shock and horror that a young woman had been brutally killed and then back to the film.

And I looked at the two police officers who were transporting me. I'd like to say they both had bad breath, dandruff, grey skin, spots, any of the things that make for villainous cops in story books. But they didn't. They were just two blokes doing a job of work, which this morning involved me. How little real life is like a story book when it comes right down to it.

We parked out back and walked to the door that I'd been through before on occasion. Blackford punched in the security code and they took me through to an interview room. 'Would you like some tea?' Hawes asked. 'You've had a rough morning.'

So he was going to be the good cop.

'Please,' I said.

He went off to get it and Blackford sat opposite me and said nothing. Bad cop.

When Hawes came back with a Styrofoam cup he was accompanied by another detective. This one I knew. And he knew me.

'Sharman,' he said nastily. 'Welcome back.'

'Sergeant Lewis,' I said. 'Long time.' It had been a long time. Years. When I'd known him last I'd been a DC at Kennington, he'd been a DS. A nasty little fucker who liked to throw his weight about and bully his subordinates. By the looks of things time hadn't mellowed him. Ladies and gentlemen, meet worst cop.

'Inspector now,' he corrected me. 'But I knew we'd meet again on the rocky road through life,' he said.

'Just our luck.'

'I thought it might be you,' said Lewis. 'When I heard your name.'

'And you just couldn't wait to put out the welcome mat, is that it?'

'Something like that.' Hawes and Blackford looked puzzled at our dialogue. 'Gentlemen,' said Lewis to them, almost rubbing his hands in glee, 'I think we should have a conference before we continue.'

The three of them left the room and a young uniform came in and stood at ease by the door. I drank their rotten tea and smoked a cigarette. The young uniform looked like he was going to be sick at the smell of smoke. They don't make coppers like they used to.

There was no ashtray so I stubbed the cigarette on the floor as the three detectives returned. The young PC looked hurt at that too. The cigarette that is. Perhaps he was part of the litter squad.

'Well, Sharman,' said Lewis when he'd dismissed the uniform. 'We need to talk.'

'My solicitor,' I reminded them.

'And who is your solicitor?' asked Blackford.

'Jerry Finbarr,' I replied. They looked at each other. They all knew his name right enough. 'And Sheila worked for him,' I added.

'Cosy,' said Lewis.

'Just circumstance,' I replied.

The three looked at me like I was some strange species they'd never encountered before.

'Can you get him for me?' I asked.

'I think we have a contact number,' said Lewis. 'Meanwhile why don't we have a little chat. I hope you have no objections.'

'I'll talk,' I said. 'I've got nothing to hide. But if it gets sticky I'll wait for Jerry.'

'Seems fair,' said Blackford. 'I'll just set up the tape recorder.'

Seventeen

ALL THREE OF them were going to sit in on the interview. Even in that part of south London there's only so many chances to get involved in a murder investigation. In fact since Brixton had turned into a sort of low-rent Notting Hill full of Bohos drinking cappuccino and eating carrot cake with no smoking in restaurants and skips outside every house, the front line seemed to have moved north of the river, in the direction of Hackney and Dalston and beyond, taking the drugs and guns with it. Not all of them of course, but enough.

I didn't mind. I wasn't under arrest and I wanted to help them catch Sheila's killer. And besides it was something to do. Something to stop me thinking about what I'd seen in her bedroom. There was plenty of time for that. There was going to be plenty of time for a lot of things. A long, long, lonely time, stretching out in front of me like a blank sheet.

Before they started, Lewis fucked off and came back with a thick, brown file. I didn't bother trying to read what it said on the front upside down, but I'd've bet it was mine. Blackford checked the tapes on the machine, gave the date, time and those present.

Hawes took the lead, which surprised me a little, but then I suppose it was meant to. 'Before we go any further, Mr Sharman,' he said, 'I'm going to caution you.'

'Do you think I did it?' I asked.

'This is just for the record, Mr Sharman,' he said.

And just in case they wanted to do me for not calling them sooner, I thought, but I didn't care. 'Then I should wait for Finbarr maybe,' I said.

'That's your privilege.'

'Isn't it just.'

'So?' he said.

'Do what you want,' I replied. 'See if I fucking care.'

So he did, and once that was sorted he said, 'Now, Mr Sharman, tell me exactly what happened this morning.'

I told him. I told him about walking round to Sheila's house and what I'd found there. I told him about calling the police and what had happened since. It didn't take long. It wasn't *War and Peace*. I tried to be as accurate about the times as possible. I should've called the coppers when I first found her, I knew that by then. But what's done is done and there's no use crying over spilt milk as my old gran would've said.

'Right, Mr Sharman,' said Blackford, taking centre stage. 'How long have you known the deceased?'

'She's got a name,' I said. 'Use it if you don't mind. She's not a piece of meat.'

'Sorry.'

Lewis frowned at Blackford's apology.

'How long have you known Miss Madden?' Blackford continued.

'Ages. I told you she worked for Finbarr. I met her in the office years ago. But we've only been seeing each other for a few months.'

'Seeing each other?' He put a question mark at the end.

'As a couple,' I said. Then looked at Lewis. 'You know, as lovers. We slept together, things like that.'

'I know what couples do,' said Lewis.

'You amaze me,' I said. 'Been to the zoo have you? Because I'm sure no human would do it with the likes of you.'

'Enjoy yourself, Sharman,' he said. 'It's later than you think.'

'We've had a preliminary time of death put at seven this morning,' Blackford interrupted. 'Where were you then?'

'At home in bed.'

'And your flat is just a couple of minutes' walk away from Miss Madden's.'

'That's correct.'

'Alone?'

'What?'

'Were you alone in bed?'

'Yes.' I almost laughed.

'So no witnesses?'

'Not even a budgie.'

'And you didn't see Miss Madden yesterday.'

'In the morning. I stayed over at her place Thursday night.'

'You parted friends?'

'Certainly. We were friends.'

'You saw a lot of her?'

'Yes. Almost every day since the spring.'

'But not last night.'

'No.'

'So what was she doing?'

'Working late.'

'And yourself?'

'Working too.'

'Doing what?'

'I was serving a summons. I'm a private enquiry agent –'

Lewis snorted at that, but I ignored him.

'It was on a builder in Brixton who didn't finish a conservatory for a client of mine.'

'And did you? Serve the summons that is?'

I nodded.

'For the tape please, Mr Sharman.'

'Yes, I served it,' I said.

'And what time was that?'

'Seven, seven-fifteen.'

'And the person you served the summons on would confirm that?'

'If you can catch up with him. He's a bit of a slippery customer. And don't tell him he's won a telly. He won't fall for that one again.'

Lewis frowned again as I gave the name and address

of the recipient of the summons, then he decided to make himself busy. 'So you didn't go round to Miss Madden's flat, sit outside in your car and maybe see her come home with another man. And you didn't wait until this morning when he left, and pop in and cut her throat.'

I almost laughed again. 'No,' I said. 'I went home after I'd done the job, had something to eat, a pizza I bought in the Norwood Pizza Express, drank a lager or two, watched something on TV and went to bed.

'I didn't go round to Sheila's, or phone, or make any kind of contact. I didn't think she was seeing anyone else. In fact I know she wasn't. We had an arrangement based on trust. I trusted her, she trusted me. And besides, if I had gone round I would've used this.' I took her key out of my pocket. 'I'd've been inside, if what you say happened happened. But it didn't. I've been seeing Sheila exclusively since the spring and her me, just like I told you. She hasn't had time to have another relationship. Nor have I. And even if she had I don't think she'd've been interested. She wasn't that kind of person'

'The officers who were first on the scene noticed that you had a little blood on your right hand. There's still some there if I'm not mistaken,' said Blackford.

I looked down at it. The smears I'd got off her body had almost gone and my fingers were steady. Too steady. I knew I'd pay for that later. 'I held her hand,' I said. 'I sat with her.'

Lewis smirked. 'Very touching,' he said. 'Why didn't you report the crime as soon as you found her?'

'I needed some time.'

'Time to get your story straight. Get rid of the weapon.'

'Give me a break,' I said. 'I've already told you I had nothing to do with it. Why aren't you out there –' I waved my hand in the general direction of the door '– finding whoever did do it?'

'If you'd been more prompt with your call perhaps we'd have some idea who did do it,' said Lewis.

'Perhaps,' I replied. 'But I doubt it.'

'You're a shit, Sharman,' said Lewis. 'You always were and you always will be. You thought you could be a one-man band when you were on the force and obviously things haven't changed. I could do you on half a dozen charges . . .'

'And enjoy yourself immensely,' I said, as a wave of tiredness and misery swept over me. 'Go ahead, do what you want. Get out the fucking truncheons for all I care, but the answers will still be the same. I went round to her place this morning, found her dead and sat with her for a little while.'

'So what do you think happened?' Blackford interrupted us again.

I pulled myself together with an effort. 'One of two things,' I said. 'Either it was a break-in that went wrong, or else someone she knew came knocking and killed her.'

'Any candidates?'

'Only one,' I said.

'And who is that?'

'Her old boyfriend. Johnny Tufnell.'

'Yes, we know Johnny,' said Blackford.

'I just bet you do.'

'What makes you think it might be him?' asked Hawes.

'He used to knock her about. She slung him out at the beginning of the year. I moved in, figuratively speaking. He was the type who'd keep his ear to the ground. Be aware of what she was up to. She was too good to lose permanently.'

'He waited for his chance,' said Blackford. 'If it was him.'

I had to agree but I said nothing. 'I'll tell you one thing,' I said instead.

'What?' Blackford again.

'Someone spun the drum.'

'What makes you say that?'

'It was a mess. But not her kind of mess. I just know.'

'Did you check to see if anything was missing?'

'For Christ's sake,' I said. 'I'd just found her dead. What do you think? I sat there and counted the spoons?'

'Did she have many valuables?' asked Hawes.

I shook my head. 'A few bits of jewellery she'd collected over the years that she liked to wear . . .' I almost lost it then, but gripped the seat until the edges bit into my palms. 'She was a clerk stroke typist stroke receptionist at Finbarr's. She didn't earn a fortune. She had the mortgage, a decent TV and video and stereo. She spent her money on clothes and CDs and going out . . .' That was all I could say.

Lewis interrupted again at that point. 'You don't have a lot of luck with women do you, Sharman?' he asked.

'Mr Sharman will do nicely,' I replied, looking him straight in the eye. 'And no, I don't.'

'They seem to die on you with almost indecent regularity.'

'Is this going somewhere?' I asked, and took out my cigarettes. I was down to my last one. 'And could you get me an ashtray?'

Lewis scowled at Hawes who got up and left the room. Blackford noted his exit for the tape.

'I think you might have killed Miss Madden,' said Lewis almost triumphantly.

'You're so full of shit, Lewis, you've got brown eyes,' I said as I lit up. 'But if this is where it's going I think I'll just wait for my brief, which is really what I should've done in the first place.'

'Inspector Lewis,' he hissed.

'You're so full of shit, Inspector Lewis, you've got brown eyes,' I corrected myself.

'Did you?' he asked. He was like a dog with a bone. A fucking Lurcher. 'Did you kill her?'

'No,' I replied. 'And let's get one thing straight, you cunt. I'm here because I want to be. Because I want to help. But you come that sort of shit with me and I'll leave unless you charge me. Now I want another cup of tea. What do you say?'

Blackford looked at Lewis, and Lewis looked back. He shook his head, told the machine what was happening and turned it off.

When it had stopped he said, 'If you call me a cunt again, Sharman, I'll have you.' By then his eyes were bulging with anger. The toys were out of the pram good and proper, and with any luck the bastard would have a heart attack and drop dead clean before my eyes.

'Get the fucking teas in, Lewis,' I said. 'That's all you're good for.'

Eighteen

THE THREE OF them went off for another little chat and left the young copper in with me again. When they came back Jerry Finbarr was with them. 'I need a conference with my client,' he said as he came in. 'In private.'

The pair of us were allowed to go into another room and left alone. The young copper showed us the way and stood outside on guard. 'Nick,' said Finbarr when the door was shut, running his hand though his hair. 'What the hell happened?'

I told him. Everything from first to last. The whole nine yards. But it didn't feel like I was talking about Sheila and me.

'I can't believe it,' he said. 'Not Sheila. I mean she's been with me for years.'

'I can't believe it either,' I told him.

'And she was so happy these last few months. I've never seen her like that before.'

'Don't Fin,' I said. 'It's bad enough as it is.'

'I'm sorry,' he said. 'You must feel dreadful.'

'Especially as that bastard Lewis is trying to pin it on me.'

'We'll soon see about that,' he said. 'Now go through it again. Every detail.'

So I did.

As I spoke he made neat notes on a foolscap pad with a gold fountain pen.

He didn't like the fact that I'd been cautioned, but he told me he could live with it. 'They're just trying to make life difficult for you, Nick,' he said.

'And they are,' I replied. 'Every minute they keep me in this dump.'

'We'll soon have you out.'

'I like your optimism.'

'That's what you're paying me for.'

'Fair enough.'

'You made a big mistake not calling the law in immediately.'

'I know. I just needed some time with her.'

'Otherwise I think you're probably in the clear.'

'I don't kill my friends or lovers, Fin,' I said. 'At least not on purpose.'

He nodded sagely, capped his pen and put it neatly onto the table next to his pad. He was like that was Fin. Very neat. Very correct. Very small and swarthy. Jewish I imagined. Not that it mattered. Or maybe Armenian or something like that. He wore an impeccable three-piece grey pinstriped suit, a white shirt, conservative tie and highly polished black shoes. 'I was at home with Betty when I heard,' he said when I'd finished. Betty was Mrs Finbarr. 'I came as soon as I could. Then I had to make my own statement.'

'When did you last see her?' I asked.

'Thursday evening. We were working late.'

I nodded my assent. I knew that.

'She told me you were working too. She said it was a miracle.'

We both smiled at that, although smiling hurt my face.

'What time did she leave?' I asked.

'About nine.'

I was sipping beer in front of the TV then.

'I asked her if she wanted to eat, have a drink, but she said she'd rather get home,' he said.

If only I'd decided to take a stroll round to her place, let myself in if she wasn't home. Wait for the sound of her feet on the stairs. I put my face in my hands and Fin got to his feet, came round the table and touched me on the shoulder. 'I could've saved her,' I said, looking up into his face.

'Maybe get yourself killed you mean.'

'At least I'd've put up a fight.'

He just nodded, pulled a face and said nothing.

'Do you think they're going to keep me here?' I asked.

'Not if I've got anything to do with it. But I wish you'd waited for me to arrive before making a statement.'

'I've got nothing to hide.'

'Since when did that stop the police railroading you into a trip to the big house.'

Fin and I share a love of American pulp crime fiction. His house is full of novels old and new and sometimes we slip into the vernacular. Even in times of stress. 'Sell me down the river you mean.'

'In one.'

'I'm glad you're here, Fin.'

'I'm always here for you, Nick, you know that.'

'So can I go home soon?'

'As soon as humanly possible.'

'It'll be a long time then, there's not much humanity in this nick it seems to me.'

'I must say you seem to be taking this well.'

'There's only two alternatives. Crack wise or burst into tears. I'd rather do my weeping in private. Or of course there's a third.'

'Which is?'

'I could get a gun and go searching for the bastard who did this and blow his head off.'

'Nick,' he said, looking round the room as if searching for hidden microphones. 'Don't mention guns in here, even as a joke.'

'Who said I was joking?'

'Just calm down.'

'OK. And it's no conflict of interest? You representing me and Sheila working for you.'

'You're my client,' he said firmly. 'And my friend. And I'll make sure you get out of here as soon as possible.'

'Lewis hates me.'

'Then you're in good company.'

'Tell me one thing,' I said.

'What?'

'Johnny Tufnell.'

'Johnny. I hate to speak ill of one of my clients, or ex-client as he is now, but . . . Sheila met him at the office you know.'

'Yeah.'

'She was only twenty-two then. Just a baby. He swept her off her feet.'

'Then knocked her off them.'

'I believe so. I tried to warn her.'

'And about me too?'

'I told her some things. But, Nick, I stopped when she told me how you treated her. She was glowing. I was happy for her. And you.'

'Thanks, Fin. Have you seen Johnny lately?'

'Not for months. He's vanished off the face of the earth. Being a good boy for a change. Gone up north I heard.'

'He might've come back,' I said.

'He might.'

'And killed her this morning.'

'Supposition, Nick. At the moment I'm more worried about you. We'll think about Tufnell later. Right now let's go back and sort out these other reptiles.'

'If they do nick me can we get bail?'

'Difficult, but not impossible. But let's cross that bridge if and when we get to it.'

The atmosphere was different when we went back into the interview room. Blackford led the questioning and Lewis kept his gob shut. Fin was very much in charge and I watched him for his nods and head shakes when I was answering.

'Did Miss Madden have any enemies?' asked the DS, going off at a tangent.

'Not that I know of,' I said. 'Apart from Tufnell. If he *was* her enemy. I don't know, it's just supposition.' I looked at Fin when I said that and he nodded in agreement.

'How about friends?'

'She didn't have many. She told me Johnny Tufnell chased most of them off years ago. Her parents were dead. She's got a sister somewhere but they didn't communicate. When we started going out we were in the same boat. We didn't mix much. She had an address book. She kept it in her bag. I never looked in it.'

'We've found that. And you can't think of any reason anyone would want to kill her.'

I told him I didn't. Apart from Tufnell of course, but we'd been all through that.

They kept on at me all afternoon and evening, with breaks for refreshment. But every time we started again I could sense that they were losing interest. Finally at around nine they left me alone with Fin and another uniform and went outside. When they came back Lewis said, 'I don't think there's much point in carrying on. You can leave now, Mr Sharman, but don't go far.'

'Don't leave the country you mean?'

'Exactly.'

'I won't. There's a funeral to go to.'

Lewis and Hawes left then but Blackford stuck around for a few minutes and pulled me away from Fin. 'I'm sorry about him,' he said, I assumed meaning Lewis.

'Old enemies,' I said.

'So I gathered.'

'Have you got anything on who did it?'

'No. I'm afraid not.'

'What about the neighbours?'

'The old lady downstairs is almost deaf and never heard a thing.'

I nodded. Once upon a time Sheila and I had been glad of that, otherwise we might've scared the old dear half to death with the noise we made in Sheila's bedroom. All at once I wished her perfect hearing. But then that might've brought her out of her front door into the arms of a killer, who having killed once probably wouldn't hesitate to kill again. She was probably better off having heard nothing.

'We've done a door-to-door but so far there's nothing there,' he went on.

'Well thanks for not nicking me.'

'You've got some friends in your corner.'

'Meaning?'

'Oh I'm sure you'll find out. We may want to see you again.'

'I'd be surprised if you didn't.'

'Well goodnight, Mr Sharman. You have my sympathies.'

And with that he left me alone to join Finbarr.

Nineteen

IT WAS ALMOST dark when Finbarr and I left the police station. The air outside was translucent with heat and the street lights were popping on like fireflies in the dusk. He asked me if I wanted to stop for a drink or a bite to eat but I just shook my head. I needed to be alone. To think. To grieve. 'Are you sure?' he asked. 'You could come back to mine.'

'And be a spectre at the feast? I don't think so. No, you've wasted too much of your weekend on me already. Go home Fin. I'll be fine.'

'If you need me you know where I am.'

'Yeah. And thanks.' We shook hands solemnly and he started the car and drove off.

He drove to the bottom of my street, where I told him to let me out and I walked the rest of the way after buying two packets of smokes from the off-licence on the corner. I had a feeling I'd be smoking a lot before morning. I let myself in my front door and wearily climbed the stairs to the top of the house. When I got to my flat door I realised someone had been there before me. The flat key that I'd given Sheila was stuck in the lock and the key ring I'd been given years ago with five gallons of petrol hung off it, complete with the key to the house door downstairs. The flat door itself was open wide. The second open door of the day. I wondered who or what was waiting inside, but to tell the truth I was too pissed off to care. I had no weapon. My guns were in the crawl space under the roof, but it would take me minutes to get them and the noise would warn any intruder that I was about. I didn't even have a car parked outside complete with handy tyre iron. Just my bare hands. I stood on the thin carpet outside the door and pondered what to do. Inside the flat was dark and it felt empty so I leaned in and flipped on the light. The single studio room was deserted but it had been spun just like Sheila's flat. I went and peered into the small bathroom but that was empty too, and I went back, retrieved the keys, shut the door and pushed things back to roughly where they'd been when I'd left. I've never been much of a housekeeper so it didn't take long. As far as I could see nothing was missing. I went and got the bottle of Jack I keep in the cupboard over the cooker and drank from the neck. Now what the fuck were they looking for? I wondered.

Then it hit me. The envelope. The envelope that Sheila had given me months before and was nestling under the slates above my head next to my pistols. That was it. It was the only thing that we could possibly have in common.

I put the bottle on the table, went out onto the landing, clambered up and opened my hidey-hole.

The envelope was still there, and so was my Detonics .45 and a silenced .22 assassin's pistol in a velcro and leather shoulder holster, bullets and spare magazines for both.

I took both the envelope and the Detonics back into my flat, checked that the seven shot magazine was full, pumped one into the chamber, left the hammer cocked and locked and set it next to the bottle.

Now my guns were my only friends. The only things I could rely on. Except for myself. I touched the .45 and felt the warmth it had picked up from the day's heat as it had lain under the roof, and took a drink and felt its warmth too as it burst in my belly like a firework display.

For one moment I felt like ending it all and I put the barrel of the gun to my temple with my finger on the trigger. That's such a scary thing to do. It's the old river's invitation. Like standing on the edge of a tall building and feeling the need to jump, so your finger starts to twitch on the trigger and you know that it would only take a few pounds of pressure to send the firing pin down on the bullet's core and that chunk of hot lead through your

cranium. But I resisted and gingerly pulled my finger out
of the trigger guard and put the gun down.

I sat then, picked up the envelope and pinched the two
thin pieces of metal that kept it closed and slid them
through the washer and opened the bag.

Inside was a smaller white envelope, a bunch of what
looked like maps and blueprints and a C90 audio cas-
sette tape.

The envelope was addressed to me.

I opened it. Inside was a single sheet of A4 sized
paper covered in Sheila's handwriting. Just seeing it there
brought it all back and my eyes filled, but I blinked back
the tears and read what she'd written:

> Dearest Nick,
> If you ever read this, something dreadful has hap-
> pened. So I pray that you never do. First off, let me
> tell you that I love you. I never thought that I ever
> would again, so even if I'm not around, at least we
> were together for some time. The best time of my life.
> Johnny and Finbarr are planning a robbery together.
> They intend to break into the vaults of a safe deposit
> company in the City. Listen to the tape. I made it at
> the office when they were having a meeting. Another
> man called Morris was there, but I don't know his other
> name. I copied the documents from Finbarr's files. All
> the details are there. Johnny knows that I know. I had to
> tell him so that he wouldn't hurt you. But he's always
> been mad so I don't know what he'll do about it. So if
> anything happens to me you know where to look.
> And if anything does, grass them up good, baby!
> Whatever happens I'll always love you like that first
> Sunday we were together.
> Sheila

Shit, I thought as I read the letter. My mate Finbarr. I
shook my head and looked through the documents. The

place was called The Allied and Irish Bank Depository and was located in London Wall on the edge of the City of London. The maps and blueprints were the sewer system that ran underneath, and the alarm system to the vaults. There was a lot of stuff to look through and I put it aside and put the tape into my stereo. Just as I was going to press PLAY my doorbell rang. It was late and I wondered if my earlier visitors had come back so I took the Detonics and slid it down the waistband of my jeans at the back then went down to the front door. Before I left the room I stuffed the maps and blueprints back into the envelope and put it into the cupboard where I kept the booze.

I switched on the porch light, but left the hall light off, opened the door and Sheila was standing on the step.

Twenty

I'VE GOT TO tell you I nearly passed out. After everything else that had happened that day, seeing her standing on the porch nearly did for me. I literally went weak at the knees and put my hand on the door frame for support.

Sheila was dead. I'd seen her with my own eyes, felt her with my own hands, kissed her cold lips with my own mouth before leaving her to the sharp knives of the pathologists. Then I saw that it wasn't her. Not quite, but almost. Her hair was a different colour. Blonde, but nearer to the mouse that was Sheila's natural colour. And it was styled differently. But her face. Her face was the one that I loved.

'Are you alright?' she asked, and it was almost Sheila's voice, but not quite again. Not so London.

'I . . . I don't know,' I stuttered.

'Are you Nick?'

I nodded dumbly.

'I'm Lucy. Lucy Madden. Sheila's sister.'

'God but you gave me a turn,' I said, and felt a cold sweat on my face and under my arms. 'You should've warned me.'

'I phoned and left a message.'

I hadn't even noticed that the machine had any messages on it. 'I didn't get it. I've been otherwise engaged.'

'Of course you have. I'm sorry, I didn't think,' she said.

'No, I'm sorry,' I replied. 'It's just that you look so much like her.'

'Do I? I didn't realise. What a bloody stupid thing to do. To just turn up without speaking to you first.'

'Don't apologise. It's been a hell of a day.'

'I know. As soon as I heard I drove down.'

'Come in,' I said, and suddenly realised I was carrying an unwanted accessory, and put my back to the wall to allow her entry and keep the gun concealed. I switched on the hall light as she came in and realised that in fact the similarity to Sheila was not as much as I'd imagined. I'd just wanted it to be her.

Lucy Madden was wearing a light macintosh over a grey suit with trousers, a cream blouse and carrying a leather shoulder bag.

'My flat's at the top,' I said, and allowed her to lead the way and pulled my shirt tails over the gun as we went. They never mention that sort of problem in books.

She went into my flat and I told her to sit. She took one of the hard chairs at the table and I sat opposite her. 'Do you want a drink?' I asked.

'Please.'

'I've only got Jack Daniel's. Unless you want tea or coffee.'

'Jack Daniel's will be fine. Do you have any ice?'

'Sure,' I said and went to the fridge. I found her ice and a glass and poured her a good triple. Then one for myself in another glass. I felt it was crass to keep drinking from the bottle in front of company.

'You found her, didn't you,' she said when she'd taken a sip and pulled a face. It's always like that with neat Uncle Jack. At least until you've had enough where you can't even feel your face any more to pull.

'Yes,' I replied

'It must've been awful.'

I was still shaky. 'It was.'

'I was in Birmingham. At home.'

'I was in the police station all day, helping with their enquiries.'

'I know. They told me.'

'You've been there too?'

'The first place I went. I tried to see you but by the time they'd finished with me you'd gone.'

'Typical.'

'I suppose.'

'Bloody coppers,' I said. 'They were wasting time with me when they should've been out looking for whoever did it.'

'It's often the person who reports a murder who actually did it.'

'Is that right?' As if I didn't know.

She nodded.

'Not this time.'

'I didn't think so. Sheila spoke highly of you.'

'I didn't know you'd been talking.'

'A little. Since she stopped seeing Johnny Tufnell. We were building bridges.'

'She didn't tell me.'

'I expect she wanted it to be a surprise.'

It was that all right. A surprise with bells and whistles. 'I'm glad,' I said.

'Me too. I wish we'd spoken more. Seen each other. But I was up there. She was down here.'

'You didn't visit?' I asked.

'I was going to. But every time we arranged a day something came up at work.'

'She was just the best person,' I said.

'She thought the same about you. She was happy. She hadn't been happy for a long time.'

'Good. I mean good that she was happy. Not that she wasn't before.'

'I know what you mean. I'm so glad she had that time with you.'

'Thanks.'

'Who do you think did it?' she asked.

I shrugged. I didn't say anything about the envelope. That was my little secret. 'Who knows?' I said, although I had a damned good idea.

'She opened the door to whoever it was. She probably knew him,' Lucy said.

She knew him all right. 'That's plod's opinion is it?' I said.

'I believe so.'

'Wonderful. Even I could have worked that out.'

'You don't seem to have a very high opinion of the police.'

'Tell me about it.'

'But you used to be one yourself.'

'Sheila told you that did she?'

Lucy nodded.

'Maybe that's why. Because I know how inept they are.'

'But at least they let you go.'

'For now. And besides, I didn't do anything.'   .

'That's what I told Inspector . . . Lewis is it?'

'That's the boy. The filth's finest. And of course he believed you.'

'I think he did.'

'And of course he'd pay attention to what you said.'

'I don't know. Apparently you told him you think Johnny Tufnell did it.'

'He told you that? Blimey, you are privileged. He normally keeps his suspicions to himself.'

'Have you got any proof?'

'No.'

'So why?'

'Why not? I think he's capable. He beat her before.'

'I know. He was the main reason Sheila and I stopped speaking.'

'You met him?'

She shook her head. 'I didn't want to.'

'You're not a bad judge. He had a bad record.'

'You've got a bit of a record yourself, Mr Sharman.'

'How do you know that? And call me Nick.'

'I did a PNC check on you.'

That one took a while to sink in. '*You* did?' I said.

She nodded again.

'How . . . ?' I said.

She reached into the shoulder bag that she'd put on the table when she came in and brought out a leather folder and flipped it open. 'Because I'm Plod too,' she said. 'Or Filth if you prefer. A Detective Sergeant, Birmingham CID.'

'Jesus,' I said, and leant back in my chair and looked at the ceiling.

Twenty-one

So THERE I was, sitting in my flat with a plainclothes copper on the day my girlfriend had been murdered, with an illegal miniature Colt M1911A1 loaded and cocked down the back of my trousers, which was just asking for five to ten years up at the big house, as Finbarr would've put it if I got caught, and just the perfect end to a perfect day. 'She never told me,' I said. 'Not a word.'

'Obviously.'

'You look too young.' A stupid thing to say.

'I'm twenty-seven, two years younger than Sheila. I've been in the Job five years.'

'And already a DS. Fast track.'

'If you say so.'

'I know so. I bet you're popular.'

'Not so's you'd notice.'

'I thought not. Things don't change much.'

'You can say that again.'

'And I take it you're the friend that I didn't know I had that DS Blackford mentioned,' I said.

'Could be.'

'Almost certainly I'd say. I didn't have many other friends in that nick today, you can count on that.'

'He told you about me?'

'No details. He just said I had someone in my corner. In a way I wish he had, it would've made it easier meeting you.'

'I'm sorry.'

'Don't be. At least you stuck up for me.'

'I had a word.'

'Well thanks for that anyway.'

'It was the least I could do under the circumstances.'

I nodded.

'Of course it doesn't mean you're off the hook totally,' she said.

'I didn't think it did, but at least I can sleep in my own bed tonight.'

'That's something.'

'So you'll've been told exactly what happened to her,' I said. 'You being one of them.'

'Some of it. They did a preliminary PM today.'

'So what's the verdict?'

'You know how she died.'

'I know that. She was cut to ribbons. But what exactly do your colleagues think happened?'

'She answered the door.'

'Early.'

'That's right.'

'In her underwear.'

'There was a bloodstained dressing gown down by the side of the bed.'

'So he took it off.'

'Looks like it.'

'Was she . . . ?' I didn't finish the question.

'Sexually assaulted?'

'Yeah.'

'No.'

'Well that's something at least. So he just got his kicks.'

'Looks like it.'

'Bastard.'

'Yes. And whoever it was really went at her with the knife. He meant it. There were cuts all over her arms where she tried to defend herself.'

'I know,' I said. 'I saw them.'

'Of course you did.'

'And they thought it might be me.'

'You're the natural suspect.'

'Of course I was. Why? Because I loved her? Because I slept with her? That makes sense does it?'

She didn't reply.

'Did they find the weapon?' I asked.

'No. But they think it was some kind of hunting knife with a serrated edge.'

'So what happens now?' I asked.

'I'll get the body released for burial as soon as possible. I can get past some of the red tape.'

'What kind of funeral arrangements are you making? I assume you're next of kin.'

She nodded. 'Mum and dad are buried at Norwood cemetery. She'd want to be next to them.'

My turn to nod again.

'I've got some leave due so I can stay down here for a bit.'

'Where?'

'I've got a room at the section house in Streatham for tonight. I'll make other arrangements tomorrow.'

'What about her flat?'

'She made a will. I get everything. I'll put it on the market. I certainly don't want any more to do with the place. If there's anything especially you'd like . . .'

I thought about it for a second. 'She had an old teddy bear. She kept it on the sofa.'

'You want her teddy bear?' She looked at me quizzically, and suddenly she looked so much like Sheila that I almost choked.

'Long story,' I said. 'I'll tell you some time maybe. But it reminds me of the first day we were together. Can I have it?'

'Of course.'

'By the way,' I said, 'how did you know where to find me?'

'Sheila gave me your address and number ages ago, when we first started talking again and you'd started going out. Just for emergencies.'

I nodded, and we sat together until we finished our drinks, and I wondered why, under the circumstances, neither of the people closest to her had once shed a tear.

Twenty-two

AFTER A LITTLE while we finished our drinks and she left. I walked her to her car and squatted down beside the driver's window as she started the engine. 'Thanks for coming,' I said.

'I'd like to say it was a pleasure.'

'I know. Let's get together soon. Anything you can tell me about what's happening with the investigation . . .'

'I'll tell you what I can, but you know it's confidential.'

'I understand. A need to know basis.'

'And you don't need to know.'

'But I'd like to.'

'I know, Nick.'

'And I'm sorry,' I said.

She frowned. 'About?'

'About those cracks earlier. You know, about the police.'

'Think nothing of it. I'm used to it.'

'But you didn't need it today. Not from me.'

She smiled. 'Apology accepted.'

'Thanks,' I said.

She put her hand on mine. 'Try and get some sleep,' she said.

'You too.'

She smiled a wry smile. 'It won't be easy.'

'Tell me about it.'

I stood then and she put the car into gear and pulled away and I watched the red tail lights vanish up the road.

I went back upstairs and sat in the same seat that I'd sat in before. The faint smell of her perfume was all that was left in the room, but she might as well be still sitting in front of me, the effect she'd had on my already battered senses. So much like Sheila, but so different. And a copper.

Sheila had neglected to mention that little fact. What a turn up for the book. A sodding copper. I almost laughed, but not quite.

Then my mind turned to other things and I retrieved the tape that Sheila had left for me in the envelope. My legacy. A letter, a bunch of papers, a tape and a teddy bear. I had a big lump in my throat as I punched the 'Play' button on the tape machine, but I swallowed it.

From the background noise and poor reproduction I imagined she'd left on the intercom from Finbarr's office to where she worked in the next room and stuck a microphone up close. But it was good enough to identify two of the voices, the ones that I was familiar with, and that was all that mattered.

It started with the sound of a door closing and footsteps muffled by carpet, and it went like this:

FINBARR: *Gentlemen. Please come in and sit. Johnny, I'm afraid I don't know your friend.*

JOHNNY TUFNELL: *This is Morris. Morris, Fin.*

FINBARR: *Morris something or something Morris?*

TUFNELL: *That doesn't matter.*

FINBARR: *Very well. How do you do Morris.*

MORRIS: (With an Australian accent.) *Hi, Mr Finbarr. Very well. How you doing yourself?*

FINBARR: *Fine. And do call me Fin. All my friends do. Drinks?*

TUFNELL: *Sure. Scotch.*

MORRIS: *Same for me.*

(The sound of bottles and glasses clinking)

FINBARR: *There you go.*

(More clinking.)

ALL: *Cheers!*

FINBARR: *Now Johnny I believe you have a proposition for me.*

TUFNELL: *Certainly. A big one.*

FINBARR: *Sounds good. How big?*

TUFNELL: *I'll let Morris tell you. He's the architect of all this.*

MORRIS: *It's a safe deposit vault in the City of London. That's as much as I'm prepared to tell you now. No names yet. I used to work there as a guard. You'd be amazed what people keep in places like that. Things they don't want anyone else to know about.*

FINBARR: *Such as?*

MORRIS: *Money. Lots of it that the taxman doesn't know about. Jewellery, negotiable bonds, drugs, weapons. You name it, Mr . . . Fin, and it's there. Sure there's a lot of crap that's just sentimental, but believe me most of it ain't.*

FINBARR: *How can you be so sure? I thought all these deposits were secret. I thought that was the whole point.*

MORRIS: *There are ways. Just trust me on this. In the vault there are over a thousand boxes. I've actually witnessed, though I shouldn't have, stacks of hard cash in some that would choke a donkey. We can empty those thousand boxes. Work it out for yourself. If there's only goods worth a grand in each that's a cool million. But there's not, Fin. There's stuff in some of those worth that much alone. I'd stake my life on it.*

FINBARR: *And how do we get in? Presumably this company has more security than just an old man with a tin whistle and a truncheon.*

MORRIS: *Security's tight. Tighter than a gnat's arse. But there are ways. I have the plans of the vault. And they're so sure that no one can get in that the place is empty outside office hours. And they're mean with it. They begrudge paying someone to sit around all night.*

FINBARR: *So we just walk in?*

MORRIS: *No way, sir. The walls of the vault are two feet thick, stressed concrete, and there's only one door that weighs about a ton and a half and it's on a time lock with absolutely no override.*

FINBARR: *Well gentlemen, that seems to let us all out. Now I have other appointments . . .*

TUFNELL: *Listen to the man, Fin.*

MORRIS: *In seventy-five, when I was barely eighteen, I was in Vietnam with the Australian army. I was what was known as a tunnel rat. Charlie had the place riddled with tunnels at the end. I went in with a Colt .45 and cleared old Charlie out. I'm a digger, man. And I can get under that vault. And that's the first weak link. The floor's old. It was built a hundred and fifty years ago, maybe more. I can tunnel up and blow a hole in that sucker easy. Then we're inside, and with the vault locked no one can get to us.*

FINBARR: *And the second?*

MORRIS: *The override on the time lock. If no one from the company can get in until it trips, once we're inside they can't reach us.*

FINBARR: *So we just dig a hole in the City of London, which right now is surrounded by a ring of steel against terrorists, and patrolled by police, and they're just going to let you.*

MORRIS: *Not exactly, but almost. Do you know what's under the City of London, Fin?*

There was no answer

MORRIS: *More tunnels than ran under Saigon in seventy-five. Sewers, conduits, cables, tube tunnels. Shit it's like a honeycomb under there. And there's one place where a disused tunnel runs right under the bank. I know, I've got the plans. It took me a while, but I got them in the end. And I've been down there and taken a look. Two weeks of digging would get us right up to the floor. One load of plastique and we're in the vault. We take in high powered drilling equipment and strip the place. Then we're out and away. Smooth as glass.*

FINBARR: *And you're an explosives expert too?*

MORRIS: *I know enough. If we couldn't get Charlie out, we blew those tunnels. I've done my share. Don't worry, I won't blow my fingers off.*

FINBARR: *What about the stuff you dig out? Surely people work in the sewers. Won't they become aware of it?*

MORRIS: *Not if we do it right. We simply dump the stuff into the main sewer. It's close and constantly running. As long as we're careful no one will suspect a thing.*

FINBARR: *You're very sure.*

MORRIS: *I've done my research. I've spent a lot of time on it. A lot of time and money.*

FINBARR: *And what happens when you blast? Don't the alarms trip?*

MORRIS: *Sure. There's motion sensors. But that's the beauty of it. All that happens is that some unlucky keyholder comes down and has a look round. The door is secure, time lock on. He figures that it's a false alarm, resets it and goes back to his missus in their warm bed. Meanwhile, we're like mice inside and as soon as we get the good word that the key holder's gone, we open those boxes one by one.*

FINBARR: *This is beginning to sound good. What do you need?*

TUFNELL: *Seed money. I've spent every penny I'd saved getting this far.We need transport, weapons, explosives, the drilling equipment and one more man at least, maybe two. We need to go on wages.*

FINBARR: *And you're going in, Johnny?*

TUFNELL: *Sure. I wouldn't miss it for the world.*

FINBARR: *And when do you plan to do this?*

TUFNELL: *In two months time on August bank holiday weekend. According to Morris the vault is sealed at four thirty on the Friday, and no one, but no one can get inside until it opens again at eight thirty Tuesday. No one but us that is.*

MORRIS: *That's the strength of it Fin.*

And that was where the tape clicked off.

So that was the strength of it eh, Fin? I thought. Good deal. August bank holiday. Just a few weeks away. Morris and his buddies were probably under the streets of the City of London even as I sat there, tunneling away like little moles.

I switched off the stereo, turned off the light, lit a cigarette and went and lay on the bed.

Someone had found out that Sheila knew what was going on. Someone knew that she'd made a tape. God knows how, but it was all that made sense. And someone she knew had come knocking that morning and killed her. Someone who looked for the tape first at her place then at mine. Someone who was on that tape. Finbarr or Johnny Tufnell. It had to be.

So I had a choice: Lay it all out for the law and let them pick the boys up. We knew where they were after all. Hey, I could even tell Lucy. That would be ironic.

Or else I could do something about it myself.

I lay awake a long time thinking about my choices.

And I thought about other things too.

As I lay there dry eyed, still wondering why the tears wouldn't come, I realised that there was a time for everything.

A time to grieve, which wasn't now.

And a time for vengeance.

A time to load up and ship out and find the men who directly or indirectly had murdered Sheila and make sure that they never did anything like that again.

And finally, as the sky lightened and birds started to sing, I fell asleep.

Twenty-three

I WOKE UP again about an hour later and my sheets were soaked with sweat. For a minute I thought that the events of the previous day had all been a dream, a terrible nightmare, but when I saw the Detonics that I'd left on the little table by the bed, I knew it hadn't been.

I rolled off the bed and wiped myself down with yesterday's T-shirt, then went to the kitchen and put on the kettle. I made a double strength black instant coffee and looked at the bottle of JD I'd left on the counter. What the fuck? I thought. Might as well get loaded early. It was going to be a tough day and I needed some help.

I chased the coffee with Jack Daniel's and lit the first Silk Cut of the many I knew I'd smoke that day, and suddenly the loss of Sheila hit me like a truck.

I felt as if my right arm had been chopped off and leant against the stove for support, and finally the tears came. I sobbed and choked for what seemed like hours, until there were no more sobs and chokes left. I wiped my face with a dish cloth, made more coffee over the dregs of the last and lit another cigarette. Then, when I was still, I went into the bathroom and stood under the shower, my pistol on top of a towel next to it, still cocked and ready to fire.

When I came out of the bathroom the phone was ringing.

It was Lucy. 'Did I wake you?' she asked.

'Chance would be a fine thing.'

'I couldn't sleep either.'

'The kettle's hot,' I said.

'I'll be with you in ten.'

Whilst I was getting dressed I switched on the local TV news. Sheila made about eight seconds between the closing of an A&E department at a hospital in north London and a cat that had eight kittens in the engine bay of a Ford Scorpio at a motorway services in Essex.

C'est la vie.

I was pulling the bedclothes together when I heard a car drive up and stop outside and I checked the window. It was Lucy.

I stashed the Detonics in a drawer, went downstairs and let her in.

Jesus, but she was like her sister. It was bloody uncanny.

That morning she was wearing jeans and a sweater, and her figure reminded me so much of Sheila's that it was all I could do not to grab a handful. Seeing her was doing me no good at all.

Whilst I was making her coffee I asked what plans she had for the day. A real stupid question I admit. It wasn't as if I expected her to tell me she was going to take a picnic up to Hampstead Heath followed by an evening at the theatre.

'Try and get into the flat I guess,' she replied. 'If they'll let me.'

'I'll come with you if you like,' I said, although I expected I'd be about as welcome as a wasp in an ice-cream cornet.

'OK,' she agreed, which meant that my PNC check hadn't covered all the bases.

'Want anything with this?' I asked as I passed her the mug of coffee I'd prepared.

She looked at the bottle of Jack and then at me. 'Starting early aren't you?'

'Just continuing where I left off a couple of hours ago. Care to join me?'

'I'll pass thanks, but don't let me stop you.'

I added a drop of the liquor to my cold coffee and knocked back a mouthful.

'Better?' she asked.

'Not really.'

I sat opposite her at the table and we lit cigarettes. 'God, I miss her,' I said.

'Me too,' said Lucy. 'Even though I hadn't seen her for years. It was just knowing that she was there. Talking to her, you know.'

'I know. She was easy to talk to.'

'Not always, believe me. There were times when we had screaming rows you could hear three streets away.'

'I believe that.'

'Too much alike you see,' she said.

'You can say that again.'

'I'm sorry if seeing me is painful.'

'Right now everything's painful. That's why Jack's here.' I tapped the bottle with my fingernail.

'Yeah,' she whispered.

'So were you going to?'

'What?'

'See her again.'

'I think so. I think we were just about ready.'

'And then this.'

'And then this,' she said.

I nodded. 'That fucking Tufnell's got a lot to answer for,' I said.

'He has that,' she agreed. 'If he did it.'

He did it alright, I thought, directly or indirectly. He, or one of that little team he'd put together with Morris, or whatever his name was, and Finbarr had done for her, a pound to a peanut. Finbarr had been with her for Christ's sake, that night, whilst I was poncing around in Brixton. She would've told him what our plans were. She was that kind of woman. If only I'd changed my mind. Jesus, why hadn't I been there?

'How the hell she got herself webbed up with a bottom feeder like that I don't know,' I remarked into the silence I'd allowed to gather. I was amazed how calm I sounded to myself when inside I was seething for revenge.

'We couldn't wait to get away from dad,' Lucy told me.

'He wasn't the easiest person to live with after mum died. I went to university on an army scholarship . . .'

'You were in the army?' I interrupted.

She nodded. 'But I couldn't settle. They didn't like it when I resigned, but there wasn't much they could do. So I went from one uniform to another and joined the Birmingham police. Sheila went into a load of bedsitters and bad relationships. Johnny was just the last and worst.'

'Not quite,' I said.

'Sorry Nick, I didn't mean . . . Oh, you know. You were so good for her.'

'She was good for me.'

'Would it have lasted?'

'I don't know,' I replied. 'As the wonderful Inspector Lewis noticed, I don't have a lot of luck with women, or them with me.'

'Is that what he said?'

I nodded.

'Bastard.'

'At least we agree on something about the police,' I said.

'She told me about that,' said Lucy.

'What?'

She seemed embarrassed. 'Your bad luck with women.'

'And now my jinx has hit Sheila.'

'You can't blame yourself for that.'

'Can't I?'

'No.'

'You'd be surprised. So has anyone found Tufnell yet?'

'Not that I know of.'

'And you'd know?'

'Oh yes. I've left strict instructions with Sergeant Blackford.' She touched her pocket. 'He's got my mobile number. If anything on Johnny Tufnell turns up, or anything else, no matter how slight, he's to ring me immediately.'

'I bet that bastard did it.'

She looked closely at me. A real copper's look. 'Do you know something, Nick? Something you haven't told me?'

Course I did, but I wasn't telling. Not then. Not to her. Maybe one day, maybe never. 'No,' I lied. 'Not a thing. Except that he'd be my favourite to go in the frame.'

'You're probably right.'

'Yes, I probably am.'

She finished her coffee and said, 'You coming then?'

I wasn't keen I must admit. I didn't fancy another trip to the murder house. 'I might not be very welcome,' I said lamely.

'I need the company,' she said. 'How do you think I feel?'

Pretty rough I would've thought, so despite my misgivings I picked up my leather jacket and followed her downstairs. I looked longingly at the drawer where the Detonics lay as we went, but left it cosying up to my clean socks.

Twenty-four

THERE WAS STILL evidence of the crime tape at the front of Sheila's place, but as the lady downstairs and the police and technicians needed egress it had been broken and trampled down. Outside the house, in the front seat of a Panda car, sat a bored looking PC drinking from a Coke can.

'A hive of industry,' I said as we turned the corner.

'I'll just check it's OK to go inside,' she said, and went to the driver's side of the police car and flashed her warrant card. The driver rolled down the window and they exchanged a few words, then he got on the radio. She came back to me and said, 'He's checking with CID.'

'Fuck 'em,' I said. 'I've got the keys.'

'Down, boy,' she said. 'You remember procedure.'

I did, but I didn't want to, and I didn't want to be here, and I particularly didn't want to go inside, but I guessed I owed it to Lucy. 'I hope you didn't mention me.'

'I didn't.'

After a minute the PC got out of the car and said, 'Sergeant. Inspector Lewis says you can go in, but don't disturb the scene. It's still sealed up there. He wants to know if you've got keys.'

She nodded. 'Nick,' she said.

I brought out the set Sheila had given me. Otherwise I suppose we'd've had to wait for Lewis or one of his minions to show up.

'I'll tell him,' said the PC, who turned to go back to the car, then turned again. 'I'm sorry about your sister,' he said, which I suppose goes to prove that not all coppers are bastards. Or maybe it was just because she was in the Job.

'Thank you,' said Lucy, and I saw that her eyes were wet. She quickly bustled up the path.

I caught her up and gave her the keys. She opened the front door and we went upstairs. Sheila's flat door was still taped up. Lucy snapped it and used the flat key to get inside. I followed her.

Inside was a mess. There were scuffs on the floor and the residue of fingerprint powder was everywhere. We went through to the living room and it looked like a herd of elephants had been through it. I looked at the bedroom door with trepidation. 'She was in there, wasn't she?' said Lucy.

I nodded.

She opened the door and went inside. I followed. The curtains had been drawn right back and the bed had been stripped down to the mattress. Once again it looked as if the room had been trampled on.

I hadn't seen such a forlorn sight in years.

'So this was her,' whispered Lucy, looking round at the few pathetic belongings on display.

I was suddenly angry. 'No,' I said. 'This wasn't her. This wasn't her at all. She was alive and this place is dead. Everything in here looks like trash because of what happened. But we had good times here. This stuff was important to her and because of that it was important to me. She wasn't rich or famous, and she didn't have much, but everything meant something to her. We laughed in here for Christ's sake Lucy. We made love on that bed and talked for hours and it meant something. She kept the curtains closed so we couldn't see the dust, but it didn't matter. But now all I can see is the dust, and I don't like it. I want to get out of here and breathe some fresh air. I'll meet you outside.' And I fled.

When I was back in the tiny front garden I lit a cigarette and sat on the wall. The PC regarded me through the windscreen of his car, and I gave a tight smile that he returned.

I'd just finished the cigarette when Lucy came out and closed the front door behind her. She walked down the path and up to me. 'I'm truly sorry, Nick,' she said. 'I didn't mean that like it sounded. It was selfish of me to bring you here after what you saw yesterday.'

'It's OK,' I said. 'I shouldn't have given you a hard time.'

'You didn't. You told the truth. Which is something I couldn't see. I was looking with a copper's eyes, not her sister's. I feel ashamed.'

'Don't,' I said.

'Friends,' she said, holding out her little hand that was the double of Sheila's.

'Friends,' I said, and took it, and held it just too long.

Twenty-five

'NICK,' SHE SAID, sitting on the wall next to me and accepting a cigarette. 'In your statement you said you thought her place had been turned over.'

'I know it had.'

'What? Like a robbery?'

I had to be careful here. 'Yeah,' I said.

'But nothing was taken.'

'Nothing that I could see, but then she had nothing. Or at least not much.'

'But if Johnny Tufnell did it why would he bother?'

'To make it look like a robbery.'

'But then why not take anything?'

A conundrum I thought. And one I knew the answer to, or thought I did. 'I don't know, Lucy,' I said. 'Who can tell what goes through someone's head who'd just done what he'd done? Whether it was Tufnell or not.'

'Yeah,' she said tiredly.

'What are you going to do now?' I asked. Partly out of interest, partly to change the subject.

'I'm going to the nick. Check in with DI Lewis.'

'Well you can definitely count me out of that one. I've seen enough of the inside of police stations lately to last me a lifetime. And enough of that shit Lewis.'

'Me too, but I've got to go. I've got to know that they're doing something. So what are you going to do?'

'I'm going to go home,' I replied. 'What are you doing later?'

'Not a lot.'

'Come round when you're finished. Fill me in on what our boys in blue have come up with. We can have dinner or something.'

'Sounds good to me.'

We walked back to my place and Lucy got into her car and drove off. Before she got into her car she reached into her shoulder bag and brought out Sheila's teddy bear. 'Is this what you wanted?' she asked.

I nodded. 'I'd almost forgotten,' I replied, taking the scruffy little toy from her.

'I didn't.'

'Now that is interfering with the crime scene,' I said.

'Against procedure you mean.'

I nodded again.

'I don't think this little fellow is going to make any difference.'

'He'll make a difference to me.'

'If only he could talk,' she said.

'If only.'

'Well, I'd better be off.'

'If you hear anything . . .' I didn't finish the sentence.

'You'll be the first to know.'

'Then take care of yourself.'

'You too. See you later.'

'Later.'

She got into her car and drove off with a wave. When she was gone I went inside.

Once there I put Teddy on the table where he could scope what was going on, then I dug out the envelope that Sheila had left me and had a closer look at the maps, plans and blueprints.

I figured that Finbarr had been right about one thing. The City of London was a high security area, under constant patrol from the security forces and dotted with CCTV cameras. Ones that could read number plates and spot stolen cars. But there again they couldn't read minds. They just recorded events and that was that.

There was one map that was particularly interesting. It showed one of the small alleys that crisscrossed the area and there was a red dot in one corner. I found my A-Z and a magnifying glass and looked it up. It was so small on the map as to be almost invisible. I would've bet my life on two things. One was that the dot marked a manhole cover of some kind, and the second was that the alley was so narrow and insignificant that no camera covered it. And I'd also bet that it was how the team was going to get in to the sewer system and away with the swag.

There was only one thing for it. At some time in the near future I was going to have to go in and make a reconnaissance.

Twenty-six

L UCY CAME BACK around six. She looked like she'd had a rough day. 'You need a drink,' I said.

'Several.'

'There's a halfway decent pub not far away. And then we can find somewhere to eat.'

'Lead me to it.'

When we were sat in the pub garden far enough away from anyone else to be able to talk privately, she told me what had occurred.

It wasn't much. Police enquiries were proceeding. There were no witnesses to anyone around the house on the morning of Sheila's murder. The murder weapon was still missing. I was out of the frame, which was a bloody relief even though I shouldn't've been in it at all, and Johnny Tufnell was wanted for questioning but had vanished. Hadn't been spotted for months in any of his old haunts. My theory was that he was currently thirty feet beneath the City of London digging his way to a fortune, but I still kept shtumm.

As the hot ball of the sun crossed the rooftops she started to chill out and around seven we went to a local Chinese for dinner. Like the pub, not one I'd frequented with Sheila. I didn't want to bump into anyone we'd known, especially with her almost double in tow which was guaranteed to cause confusion.

It was the usual sort of cheap Chinese that abound in south London, a bit too much salt in the meat, the vegetables weren't cut up small enough, but the portions were large and they were licensed. By the time we'd finished, the food bill was about eight quid and the booze was about fifty. Lucy insisted on paying and I let her, and after she'd settled the bill we walked unsteadily back to my place with her hanging on to my arm like a limpet.

We went into my flat and I got out a fresh bottle of Jack.

'I shouldn't,' she said.

'Nor me,' I agreed. 'But I'm going to. Join me?'

She let me pour her a glass and we toasted each other as Sonny Rollins did his thing on the stereo.

'I need to do a pee,' she said, and got up. It was almost too much like the first time I'd ever been properly alone with Sheila, and I'd had too much to drink that evening. I grabbed Lucy by the wrist as she passed my chair and stopped her.

She turned and looked at me and there was a look of contempt on her face. 'So what's this?' she asked. 'Going for second best?'

I shook my head. 'No,' I said. 'I didn't mean . . .' But I did. I did mean, and I didn't give a shit what she thought of me.

'Don't give me that, Nick,' she said. 'What's the idea? You jump the sister, close your eyes and think of Sheila while I close my eyes and think of England? I don't think so, do you?' And she snatched her wrist out of my grasp.

I should've apologised, been contrite, but I was too pissed and feeling sorry for myself. The most loathsome of emotions. So instead, when she came back I said, 'So what's the problem? You married?'

She shook her head. 'No. But I do have a partner.'

'A partner,' I said. 'Your fucking partner. I hate that word. Your husband or your wife. Your boyfriend or your girlfriend. Your bloke or your bird. That's OK. But your fucking partner. No. Your partner is someone you go into business with. Or crime. Or tennis. Or fucking bridge even. So what is he? Your partner? Another fucking copper?'

'No he's not a copper. In fact he's not even a he.'

It took a minute to sink into my booze-addled brain.

'For fuck's sake,' I said. 'I don't believe it.' I shook my head. 'Well that just puts the tin lid on the whole fucking affair. A fucking dyke. Are you kidding me? You're a fucking dyke?' I laughed, but the sound was suspiciously like a death rattle and not funny at all.

She looked at me and nodded.

'Well, Jesus Christ,' I said. 'It sure don't run in the family.'

Twenty-seven

LUCY DIDN'T PUNCH me in the mouth at that, but if she had I wouldn't've blamed her. Instead she called a cab from a number on one of the cards by the phone, her face like thunder, and ignoring my slurred apologies she left the flat and waited for the taxi downstairs in the street, as I watched from my window. After it had come and she'd gone, I finished the new bottle of Jack then collapsed into bed.

I woke up with the birds, in a tangle of sheets and a head like a foundry on overtime, and groaned aloud.

'Jesus,' I said to myself. 'You really blew it this time.'

See, I remember everything, however drunk or stoned I get. Total recall. No convenient blackouts for me. I don't believe people who say they don't remember. To me that's just a way of avoiding responsibility for your own actions. Me, I'm responsible for every lousy thing I've ever done.

I rolled off the bed and took myself and my mouth, which tasted like the inside of an old sock, to the bathroom.

'Christ,' I said when I looked at myself in the mirror, where I resembled something from The Hammer House of Horror. 'What the fuck are you doing to yourself?'

I cleaned my teeth, shaved and showered, found clean clothes and made a pot of tea and some toast, but I couldn't face the food without heaving, so I just sipped at the boiling brew. There was one Silk Cut left in a packet on the table. I smoked it over my second cup.

The phone rang then. My stomach turned as I picked it up. What now? I thought.

It was Judith. 'Is it true?' she asked without preamble.

'What?'

'Sheila.'

'It's true. How did you find out?'

'Jerry's dad phoned him. He saw it on TV. He remembered her name. And yours.'

'I was mentioned was I? I've stopped watching TV.'

'What happened, Dad?'

'She was murdered.'

'Knifed, he said.'

'That's right.'

'Christ! You and knives.'

'What?'

'The restaurant that night we came down.'

I'd forgotten all about that. 'What can I say, Judith?'

'I don't know, Dad. Your life.'

'It was nothing to do with me?'

'Are you sure?'

And of course I wasn't. Could it have been someone from my murky past getting revenge at last? 'I'm not sure of anything right now.'

'She was so nice.'

'I know.'

'I really thought you two might make a go of it.'

'So did I.'

'I'm so sorry, Dad.'

'Thanks.'

'Do you want me to come down?'

'No. Stay as far away from all this as possible.'

'Were you even going to tell me?'

'No. Yes. Of course I was. I was just waiting for the right time.' I felt a stab of conscience. I hadn't even thought of Judith over the last few days. 'It's bloody difficult, love.'

'How could something like that happen? She seemed like a good person.'

I gripped the side of the table. 'She was.'

'So how?'

'I don't know.'

'If there's anything I can do . . .'

'I don't think so, sweetheart.'

'When's the funeral?'

'I don't know. Her sister's here. She's handling things. They have to release the body.'

'Let me know and I'll send some flowers.'

I nearly wept again at that. 'That'll be nice.'

'Are you sure you don't want me to come?'

'Quite sure. There'll be press I expect. I don't want you involved.' Judith had been involved once before in one of my escapades and I didn't want her going through that again.

'OK, Dad.'

'How's Jerry?'

'Fine.'

'What he must think of me?'

'He likes you.'

'Well that's something.'

'And so do I. I love you, Dad.'

'The feeling's mutual.'

'I know. If you need to talk . . .'

'You'll be the first person I call.'

'Good. I'll talk to you soon.'

'You will.'

And with that we both said farewell and hung up.

I went over to the window and looked outside and saw that Lucy's car was still parked in front of my house, and as I was standing there an old Honda with a cab radio aerial stuck on the roof pulled up and she stepped out.

I ran downstairs and caught her as she got into the car. 'Lucy,' I said. 'Listen. I'm sorry about last night.'

'Morning-after remorse?' she asked.

'I know I was drunk.'

'Extremely drunk.'

'Yeah. Extremely. But I didn't mean . . .'

'Didn't mean what? Trying to force yourself onto me or to belittle my sexual preferences.'

'Come on, Lucy,' I said. 'Don't go all PC on me. I didn't try and force myself on you. You got the wrong end of the stick.'

'And?'

'Well OK, I belittled your sexual preferences, but I just didn't expect . . .'

'What? That I bat for the other side? Dance at the other end of the ballroom? Isn't that how you boys so graciously put it?'

'Well, you know . . .'

'Don't you think I have to put up with snide remarks at work? And why do you think I quit the army? I've heard them all, Nick. "All you need is a fuck by a real man and you'll be cured." You know the sort of thing.'

I did.

'I've had the notes left on my locker, and photographs of cocks left on my desk, and men who should know better trying to put their hands up my skirt.

'But I expected more from you. Sheila led me to expect more.' And all of a sudden she was crying.

I put my arm around her and said, 'Come on upstairs. I'll make tea.'

She allowed me to lead her into the house and up to the flat, where she sat at the table whilst I reboiled the kettle, and she dried her eyes with a bunch of tissues I gave her.

'Christ, but this is a lousy job,' she said. 'No wonder you got out.'

'I was given a helping hand,' I explained. 'But you must know that.'

She nodded and dropped the Kleenex in the bin, sniffed and blinked.

'Better now?' I asked.

'Don't patronise me, Nick,' she said angrily.

'Jesus, I can't do anything right, can I?'

She smiled. 'You're on probation. Let's leave it at that. And I got a message this morning. They're releasing

Sheila's body tomorrow, so I'm going to arrange the funeral.'

On which happy note I put a couple of tea bags into the pot and poured on the hot water.

Part Two

To Babylon By Bus

Twenty-eight

S HE STOPPED AND talked for maybe an hour. She told me
something of her and Sheila's childhood. Not an idyllic
one by all accounts. 'We were rivals from the beginning,'
she said. 'When Sheila was five and I was three, she took
me down to the police station in her doll's pram and told
them she'd found me in the street. Mum and Dad went
potty. It may seem funny now,' she added, seeing the look
on my face, 'but it wasn't then.'

'But that's where you ended up anyway.'

'Yeah.'

I asked what had happened to their mother and father.
Sheila had told me they were dead but left it at that. I
hadn't enquired further. It seemed she didn't want to talk
about it, so I hadn't pressed her.

'Mum had cancer. Dad just curled up and died after
she went. He didn't last two years.' Then she went on
to explain how the two girls had drifted apart after that,
before the arrival of Johnny Tufnell had made the rift more
permanent.

'He's got a lot to answer for, that bloke,' I said.

'It wasn't just him. We were so stubborn. It's a family
trait.'

'Tell me about it.'

'But I'm glad neither of them is here to see this.'

I agreed with a nod.

'I'm all alone now,' she said. 'A real orphan. Sounds silly
at my age, doesn't it?'

'No.'

'I'm glad you're here, Nick,' she said, covering my hand
with hers. 'I couldn't face all this totally alone.'

'What about your . . .'

'My partner? Sorry, I know you hate that word. No. She

didn't know Sheila. I don't think they'd even spoken. It didn't seem right to get her involved. I suppose she would've done if I'd asked, but this was something I had to face on my own. Apart from you of course,' she added with a smile. 'Listen, I've got to fly. I've still got stacks of things to do.'

'Need a hand?'

'No. But it's been good seeing you. We'll get together soon.'

'Fine,' I said, and she left me with a kiss on the cheek.

After she'd gone, I decided that that was the day to take my first recce round the City. I took the Mustang up as far as the South Bank, parked it in an NCP and caught a bus over the river to the financial district. I didn't want any film of my motor on record. It was too memorable.

I got off the bus on London Wall and went looking for the alley that had been marked on the map Sheila had left me.

It was easy to find, a tiny blind thoroughfare between two slightly wider alleys that led from London Wall to Moorgate. And bang on the corner of the main roads was The Allied and Irish Bank Depository. Bingo.

And guess what? Just where the red dot had been on the map was an iron manhole cover, giant size.

And guess what again? There was no sign of a CCTV camera in that alley. It all fitted.

But even without a camera I didn't linger, just carried on strolling with the lunchtime crowds of office workers that I'd used as camouflage until I reached the edge of the City again, and found a quiet little boozer and had a couple of pints to placate the army of hobnailed booted infantry who were still marching around inside my head before walking back to where the car was parked.

I got back home around three-thirty and there was a message on my machine from Lucy. She'd had to go back to Birmingham, but would be back in London the day after next and she'd come round. The funeral was to be the day after that – Thursday. Pretty swift for a murder investigation. But Sheila was going to be buried so they could always dig her up again. An awful thought, but the truth. Lucy didn't tell me why she'd gone back to the Midlands. Maybe it was something to do with work, or maybe she couldn't wait to get back to her partner and get down and dirty with a real woman.

I opened the bottle of JD I'd bought in the off licence at the bottom of the street, put Stan Getz on the stereo, toasted the world and jumped back into the bottle.

When almost half the booze was gone I fell asleep and dreamed of Sheila.

She was alive and well, no blood, no knife slashes on her hands or arms or throat. I know that worried me, but I couldn't think why. We were walking hand-in-hand down a wide, hot boulevard like something in the south of France. She was dressed in a little, flower-patterned, floaty summer dress and she was laughing. But what she was laughing at I didn't know. I think that worried me too.

She looked so cute and pretty there walking next to me that no one could blame me for loving her. Her hair was clean and fresh and her skin was tanned and smooth, and she just seemed to float down that street like she'd never get old, which she wasn't going to, but I'm not sure if I was aware of that in the dream, or I just thought about it later.

Then we went into a railway station. I'm pretty sure that was significant. It was a French railway station too, like I remembered from some holiday when I was a lot younger, although Sheila and I had never been abroad together. But we'd promised to. To just vanish for a few weeks, away from where anyone knew us, and pretend we were anyone else apart from who we really were. Inside the vast station I could smell coffee and French cigarettes, and the rays of the sun that came through the glass roof were full of pieces of dust that were as bright as crystal.

Sheila told me she'd forgotten something and that I

must wait exactly where I was, not to move or else she might not be able to find me again, which of course she couldn't, but that didn't occur to me either. She jumped up and kissed me on the cheek, let go of my hand and moved away through the crowds that filled the concourse with just a glance over her shoulder, a heartbreaking smile on her lips. I watched the skirt of her dress twitching over her bottom as she moved through the people, dodging gracefully between the porters and the passengers until she vanished without another backward look.

How long I waited in my dream I don't know, but it grew dark and cold and the crowds thinned and there was no sign of her. I knew that if I moved from where she'd left me I'd never see her again, but I also knew that there was something badly wrong and I needed to go and find her.

I was suddenly terrified and I tried to run in the direction she had gone, but like in so many of my dreams my legs wouldn't obey me, and the faster I tried to go the further the walls of the station seemed to move away. I panicked then, and could feel the tears well up in my eyes, as much tears of frustration as sorrow.

And then I saw her. I wiped the tears away and there she was, standing at the entrance to one of the platforms talking to a shadowy figure and I noticed that she was carrying a huge bunch of white roses. I tried to call out but nothing came out of my mouth, and she passed through the entrance and out of my sight. I tried to run faster and call again, but all I could hear was the sound of my own breath rasping in my ears. Eventually, although it seemed like years had passed, I got to the barrier, only to see the last carriage of a train snaking its way past the far end of the platform, which was deserted except for a single white rose lying in the dirt.

I woke up in the dark, real tears drying on my cheeks,

and I think I actually shouted her name before I remembered where I was and what had happened, and I reached for the bottle again and lay there with my heart beating so loudly it sounded louder than any shout ever could.

Twenty-nine

I KNEW I wouldn't go back to sleep, or maybe I was frightened to in case I dreamt about her being alive again, and the terrible disappointment I would feel when I woke and found it was all a lie. So I just lay there for the rest of the night, drinking and smoking, watching the bone white moon move across the sky over the houses opposite through the open curtains, and thinking about all the empty places in my heart where Sheila had lived and what I was intending to do to the people who had snuffed out her life. It was the only thing that kept me sane as that long night dragged through to morning.

It was another beautiful day, but I could see no beauty in it. For all I cared, if the sun had not come up at all it would have made little difference to the way I felt. I got up, made a desultory toilet and drank three cups of coffee. By eight I'd done everything I had to do and the day stretched in front of me like a blank white page. By eleven I was climbing the walls and decided to go for a drink. I wandered from one pub to another, watching them gradually fill and empty as the day went by. I spoke to no one but the staff as I went. I wasn't in the mood for convivial saloon bar chat. I started on pints, then after four or five, when I began to feel bloated, I changed to large brandies with Coke and ice. I sat outside whenever I could, feeling the sun hot on my face and watching the world go by. I saw beautiful women and handsome men seemingly without a care in the world, laughing, enjoying the weather, and the more fun they had the less I did. When I wasn't on licensed premises I walked the streets feeling as alone and lonely as I'd ever felt in my life. The day waxed and waned around me, and when the final barman in the final pub called last orders I drank up and walked home. I arrived there around midnight, not able to remember one of the pubs I'd visited and who I'd seen. I fell into my unmade bed and finally slept the sleep of the dead. I think I dreamt about Sheila again, but thankfully I couldn't remember the details when I woke up.

Wednesday was the same, but as I was expecting a visit from Lucy I stayed closer to home. She eventually called at around four and told me she wouldn't be back until the morning. Something had come up. She didn't explain and I didn't ask. The funeral was set for noon and she told me she'd see me there. I spent the evening with my friend Jack Daniel's and a lot of repeats on TV.

I was up with the sun again on Thursday. I drank my breakfast from the bottom of the bottle I hadn't managed to finish before falling asleep in front of the box the night before, and ironed my last clean shirt. I dressed in the same suit I'd worn for my first night out with Sheila, and walked to the cemetery, stopping at a couple of pubs on the way. I must've drunk enough to kill an Irish navvy that night and morning, yet I swear I was sober when I got to the cemetery. I walked up the long hill from the main road to the little chapel where Sheila's service was going to be held, and the flowers bloomed and the little birdies sang in the treetops, and the sky was as blue as blue could be, and the sun shone brightly again, but I felt like there was a black cloud all over the world.

Thirty

THE FUNERAL WAS a godawful affair. But what funeral isn't? And I've been to enough for two lifetimes. More.

There were only four of us in the small chapel. Five if you count the vicar. Six if you count the deceased. Outside there was one reporter from the local paper. We all ignored him.

I was there, Lucy was there, DS Blackford was there, and Finbarr was there, and it took me all my self control not to tear out his lungs and feed them to him bit by bit.

The vicar, who had never met Sheila, intoned some words that were supposed to be comforting, but in fact were meaningless, and the sun shone through the stained-glass windows on the righteous and the unrighteous, the quick and the dead. The place smelled of damp, incense, fresh flowers, dead flowers, sorrow and pain. And if you don't know what sorrow and pain smell like you should've been standing next to me looking at the plain wooden box that Sheila had ended up in.

When the short service was over we all walked to the graveside where the undertaker's men deposited Sheila's remains into the grave, the vicar read from his little black book, Lucy, Finbarr and I threw dry dirt onto the box, and I put in a bouquet of white roses similar to those that Sheila had been carrying in my dream, that I'd bought from the stall just inside the cemetery gates on my way in.

And that was where another chapter in my life closed.

DS Blackford kept his distance, only coming over when the funeral was done to say a few more empty words to which I didn't listen, just nodded as a response. He shook Lucy's hand and left. Why he'd come God knows. Maybe he'd expected me to make a confession over her coffin as it was lowered into the ground. Or maybe he'd expected Johnny Tufnell to turn up to see the final instalment of his ex-girlfriend's life and Blackford could clap on the handcuffs. Whichever it was he was disappointed. Of course it could have been that he'd come out of sheer humanity at the death of another human being, but right then I wasn't in the mood to credit that.

Finbarr, Lucy and I stood there in an awkward silence as we watched him walk down the hill, and the small earth moving machine trundled across the grass getting ready to fill in the hole. Finbarr suggested that we all go for a drink and I could hardly refuse without letting the cat out of the bag. So Lucy and I got into her car, after she'd put some more flowers on her parents' graves, and drove to Dulwich Village where there was a boozer with a big garden. Finbarr followed us in his Jaguar. At that time of day the pub was almost empty. Finbarr bought a round and we took the drinks into the open air. On the drive over I don't think Lucy and I exchanged more than half a dozen words.

'This has been one of the saddest days of my life,' Finbarr said as we drank, and I almost believed him.

'Thanks for coming,' said Lucy.

'I could hardly not,' he replied. 'We'd known each other for years.'

Or maybe you just had to make sure she's dead, I thought.

'Any progress?' he asked.

'On catching whoever did it?' said Lucy.

He nodded.

'Not so far.'

'Jesus,' I said. 'Do we have to?'

'Sorry, Nick,' said Finbarr. 'I wasn't thinking.'

I put my head in my hands and Lucy touched my shoulder.

'Anyone for another drink?' asked Finbarr.

He bought another round and stayed for about an hour,

before he told us he had to get back to the office. 'More clients to see,' he said as he stood to leave. 'I'll catch up with you later,' and he solemnly shook both our hands.

'More crims to let back on the street more like,' said Lucy, as he walked across the grass away from us.

'That's showbiz,' I said.

'I don't know how you can stand having him around.'

'You get used to it.'

'I never could.'

'You'd be amazed what you can get used to.'

'Tell me about it. I thought Brum was bad, but this place.'

'But you were brought up round here.'

'But it's changed since I left. And not for the better.'

'I won't argue about that.'

We sat in silence for a few minutes, both staring into our drinks. 'So what now, Nick?' she asked.

'What, today? Or all the todays to come?'

'Both.'

'Today I intend to get righteously loaded.'

'And then?'

'And then I suppose I'll just get on with my little life. What about you?'

'Back to Birmingham tomorrow, and the same I imagine.'

'And today?'

'Maybe I'll join you, if you'll let me.'

'A wake, huh?'

'If you like.'

'Sounds acceptable,' I said.

'I think Sheila would've liked that.'

'Me too,' I agreed.

'So shall we?'

'I'd be honoured.'

'Good,' she said. 'I'm glad.'

'Listen, before we start, I just want to say that I'm

really sorry about the other night. I was bang out of order.'

'Forget it.'

'I can't. I said some shit and I poked my nose into things that weren't my business, and I made a fool of myself. Your life is your life. Christ knows I'm the last person who should be judging others. And you've gone though as bad a time as me over the last week or so. I should've been supportive, but instead I trampled all over your feelings like a mad bull. We buried your sister today. We buried someone you loved and someone I loved. We should stick together.'

'Nick. You were drunk and you were hurting. You needed some comfort and I could've given it to you. Instead I got on my high horse and took out a lot of things on you that I should save for the men who've given me a hard time at work. It's just that you reminded me of them.'

I went to speak but she held up her hand.

'No. Listen. I know you're not like them. I know that you were just hitting out at whoever was closest. Sheila told me things about you I imagine you wouldn't want anyone else to know, and I'll respect that. She loved you, Nick, and I know you loved her. I think you two might have stuck together for a long time. Maybe forever. In fact you did. Her forever. Unfortunately yours has to go on. I'm just so sorry that you've lost her.' She looked at me and smiled, although her eyes were full. 'And that's the end of the speech. Sheila wouldn't want us to be like this. She'd want us to have a day to remember. Not for what we just did up at the cemetery. But for what we're going to do. So let's get some more drinks in and liven up this party.'

'Seems like a good idea,' I said. 'In fact I'll drink to it.'

'And I'll drink to you.'

We raised our glasses to each other like old friends.

'So did you have a good time in Birmingham?' I asked.

'Does anyone ever have a good time in Birmingham? It was OK. I had a few things at work to clear up and I saw my . . .' She stopped embarrassed.

'Your partner,' I added for her. 'Come on, I thought we'd been through all that.'

'Sure,' she said.

'What's her name?' I asked.

'Georgina. She's a nurse.'

I couldn't resist it. 'Sister George,' I said.

'Don't push it.'

So I left it at that.

'Do you believe in God?' she asked me after a minute.

I shook my head. 'No,' I said. 'At least not a benevolent old boy with a long white beard.'

'What then?'

'I don't really know.'

'What do you think happens?'

'When?'

'When you die.'

'Do I believe you go in front of Saint Peter with his big old book that lists all your credits and debits do you mean?'

She nodded.

'I hope not,' I said. 'Or I'll go straight to hell.'

'Me too.'

'I doubt it.'

'You don't know.'

'No I don't.'

'So what do you think happens?'

'I think you just go to sleep.'

'That's nice.'

'Not if you dream it isn't,' I said.

And on that happy note we had one more drink there, then took her car back to my place and got a cab up west. I didn't want to spend the day round Tulse Hill, and there were places that Sheila had told Lucy we went to and she wanted to see some of them.

It turned into a massive pub, club and restaurant crawl. We wandered through Mayfair and Soho, dropping into this bar here and that bar there. We ate at an Italian trattoria that probably hadn't changed since the fifties, dining on spaghetti vongole and cassata with brandied figs, and drank in clubs that thought they were so out there that the new millennium hadn't happened yet. We drank beer and gin and tequila and brandy and red wine and white wine and cocktails of every colour of the rainbow, and we toasted Sheila with every round. At some point we fell in with a couple of actors who Lucy recognised from one of the soaps, and who seemed to have cornered the London market in cocaine, and Detective Sergeant Lucille Madden of the Birmingham CID snorted her fair share in a chrome and mirrored gentlemen's toilet in a hotel where the Queen Mother had stayed. Afterwards she showed them her warrant card and they went as white as the Charlie, and she laughed and I joined in and eventually they did too. But they split pretty quickly after that. I don't blame them.

Finally at around two in the morning we landed up in Gerry's club under Shaftesbury Avenue. We danced together to Dean Martin's greatest hits under the gaze of a hundred or more reprobate actors and writers whose photographs covered the walls. Then we called another cab and headed back to south London before the boss threw us out.

'I haven't always batted for the other side,' she told me through kisses that tasted of Rémy Martin and Marlboro Lites in the back of the cab.

'I'm glad to hear it,' I said.

'I want to come home with you.'

'That's where the man's taking us.'

Once inside my flat we undressed each other and crawled under my duvet. But it wasn't right. She wasn't Sheila and I wasn't Georgina. As the sun came up she asked me one question over and over again as she tried to make

a man of me with little success. 'What do you know?' she
asked me. 'What do you know about who killed Sheila?'

But I had as little answer as I had desire and eventually
I fell asleep.

When I woke up she was gone.

No goodbye kiss, no note, no nothing.

Thirty-one

NOT THAT I'D really expected any acknowledgment of what we'd done, because, frankly we'd done nothing. It had just been like my first night with Sheila. But some recognition of who I was would've been nice. But I have found in my life that that is often what women are like.

I lay in bed the whole day, nursing the hangover from hell and working out what I was going to do next.

It was simple really. I was going to wait until the bank holiday, which was just a few days away, and go into the sewer and tunnel system under the depository and find Johnny Tufnell, Morris and whoever else was with them, and kill them. And before or after that I was going to sort Finbarr.

Then I was going to come home and take a bunch of roses up to Sheila's grave.

Blood red ones this time. For revenge.

But it wasn't going to be easy.

I'd been running the plan through my mind for days, surviving on just a few hours' sleep a night.

The main problem was that I didn't know what went on underground.

Sure, I had the maps and plans, but I'd never been in a sewer system in my life and I didn't know what I'd find down there.

Or who exactly.

Surely, if the security forces were so much in evidence above ground, they must send patrols down below. And what about the engineers who kept the sewers running? From time to time they must sweep through for a look see. For all I knew there might be armies down there.

Or on the other hand it might be deserted.

I was tempted to go down myself before the weekend,

but if something went wrong and I was spotted by either the good guys or the bad guys, I might blow the whole thing.

It was a quandary. Another bloody conundrum.

But in the end I decided to wait until the weekend and take my chances by going down blind.

Hell, it wouldn't be the first time, or probably the last.

But before I did anything, just in case I didn't come out of that maze of tunnels under the city alive, I went down to the cemetery in Greenwich to visit my late wife Dawn, my unborn child Daisy, as she would have been christened, and Dawn's best friend and latterly mine, Tracey.

I drove down in the Mustang, parked outside, bought flowers at the gate as was my habit and walked up to their gravesides overlooking the Thames and east London beyond.

Flowers. It always seemed to come down to flowers. And graves. And memories best forgotten that just wouldn't go away.

As I climbed the hill through the silence of a weekday, except for the sound of children playing somewhere beyond the walls of the graveyard, it seemed to me that instead of the empty space I'd expected, it was crowded with people standing close together on top of the burial mounds and on the grass verges and paths between them.

As I got closer I felt the air grow cold, and when I peered through slitted eyes I saw that I knew all these people, standing mute before me.

Dawn was there, with Daisy on her hip – Daisy, who had been so cruelly cut out of her body at the post-mortem. Next to them was Trace. Behind them my late friend Charlie dressed in his usual sheepskin jacket. At his side was my first wife Laura, her husband and son who had died in a plane crash over the frozen north of America.

My father, mother and brother were there, mere shades against the tree line. And people I also knew were dead, although often I didn't remember, or had never known their names. I knew they were dead because I had killed them myself, sometimes with a gun, sometimes with my bare hands.

I stopped in mid-stride, my hands shaking so much that I dropped the flowers.

What were they telling me? I wondered.

Was it my turn to join them on that long journey from the living to the dead?

I sank to my knees then, not sure if I was mad or sane, awake or asleep, and slowly the ghosts turned and vanished one by one without a backward glance until only Dawn and the baby were left, and then she too turned and left and I was alone.

My eyes were full of tears, and when I looked up again there was a small boy I didn't know regarding me with a bemused look on his face.

Suddenly his mother appeared on the path, stopped dead, looked at me with fear in her eyes and shouted, 'John. Come away this minute.'

After a long moment he turned and walked to her. She gathered him up in her arms and fled.

Thirty-two

I DECIDED THAT Sunday was the best day to go. If what I'd heard on the tape was right, the gang would be inside the vault by then, and as it was the bank holiday weekend I assumed that any workers inside the sewers would be down to a bare minimum. Also, if the explosion to get inside the vault had alerted the bank security, presumably that would've been on Saturday, so all should be serene.

Of course the whole damned thing could've fallen through and I could be left with my thumb up my arse wandering the sewers under the City looking for phantom robbers.

But whether or not it was happening, I'd need a car, the Mustang being far too distinctive to be anywhere near a big robbery, or anywhere near CCTV cameras for that matter. And I knew exactly where to get one, or at least I hoped I did.

And I had to find out where Finbarr was going to be.

On Saturday morning, which dawned clear and hot again and boded well for the holiday, I took a cab over to Notting Hill Gate and got the cabbie to drop me off a couple of blocks short of my destination, which was a cafe/restaurant called Bunters, very ethnic and popular with the crustier kind of local trustafarians, all face furniture, joints of skunk and charge accounts at Harvey Nichols. I'd phoned ahead and arranged a meet.

Of course it was carnival weekend and the place was packed out with punters ready to join in the festivities. All those good times to come meant nothing to me as I shouldered my way through the crowds, but somehow the mass of humanity made me feel more anonymous, and more certain that I would complete my task and get the clearance I needed.

Sitting in his usual cushioned seat in the furthest, darkest corner between a pair of giant speakers pumping out 'Daddy Was A Rolling Stone' by the Temptations, which by the look of some of the patrons was probably not far from the truth, was my little chum Cedric, known to his confidantes, of whom I was one, as Ricky. Next to him was a dreadlocked white girl whose slim neck seemed hardly strong enough to support the amount of metal stuck through her ears, nose, lips, cheeks and when she opened her mouth, I noticed, her tongue.

I slipped into the painted kitchen chair opposite where Ricky and pal seemed to have taken up residence, choc-a-bloc as their perches were with cigarettes, Rizlas, rolling tobacco, a couple of mobiles, music and style magazines and newspapers, ancient articles of clothing and a very new looking laptop computer which seemed to be scrolling the price of marijuana on seven continents. 'Handy, the Internet,' I said as I helped myself to one of Ricky's Marlboros.

'A boon, Mr S,' he replied, in an accent that ran the gamut from Surrey, to Stepney to Trenchtown, Jamaica.

'Aren't you going to introduce me?' I asked, nodding in the direction of the young woman at Ricky's side.

'Sorry. Veronica Mr Sharman, Mr Sharman Veronica. She's cool.'

That meant I could speak in front of her.

But first there were formalities to be observed. 'Something to drink?' I asked.

Ricky nodded, considered and replied. 'Nurishment. Banana flavour.' Veronica nodded her agreement.

I waved over the waitress, who was as heavily armoured as Ricky's lady friend, and ordered two glasses of the West Indian milk drink and a coffee for myself. 'Something to eat?' I inquired of the pair.

'Cake,' said Ricky and Veronica in tandem

'Cake,' I said to the waitress.

She nodded, obviously aware of their confection of choice.

'Got a bacon sandwich?' I asked, which apparently was something similar to requesting 'The Wearing of the Green' at a Belfast apprentices march.

'No meat,' said the waitress curtly.

'Cheese sandwich?'

'Non dairy.'

How the fuck can you have non dairy cheese? I wondered, but nodded anyway. I wasn't even that hungry.

'Any particular kind of bread?' she asked.

I just knew they wouldn't have Mother's Pride medium white sliced. 'As it comes,' I said. 'And whatever cheese you've got.' I wasn't in the mood to be picky.

The waitress went away and Veronica said, 'How can you eat meat?'

'Easy,' I replied. 'Stick it in my mouth and chew.'

'Ron's a vegan,' said Ricky.

I wasn't surprised. 'A bacon sandwich never hurt anyone,' I said.

'Except the pig it came from,' said Veronica, which I suppose was fair comment.

When the food and drinks arrived and they'd dipped their beaks into the Nurishment, and I'd examined my soft cheese sandwich on tomato and nut bread and declared it eatable, Ricky said, 'So what can I do for you this morning?'

'I need a motor,' I said. 'Something a doctor would drive. You know, unremarkable but shiny.'

'When?'

'Now.'

'Got any dough?'

'Would I come without?' I asked. 'How much?'

'Two hundred and fifty.'

Seemed fair. 'But I don't want to have wires hanging down. I'd like a set of keys.'

'Three hundred.'

I reached into my pocket and fished out three bundles of five twenty pound notes and slid them under my plate. Ricky grinned and helped himself to the other half of my sandwich and the cash vanished with the food. 'Got just the thing,' he said. 'I'll be back in a minute,' and he left me alone with the lovely Veronica.

She said nothing, just drank her drink and read last Sunday's property section of the *Times* until Ricky came back. She was probably looking for a little pied-à-terre off Portobello Road. 'It's outside,' he said.

'That was quick,' I remarked.

'You were in luck. I found a nice Mondeo just last night.'

'Before it was lost?'

'Course. It was being MOT'd down the road.'

'Plates?'

'Good as gold. It'll be safe for at least a week.'

'That's plenty.'

'Come on then,' said Ricky, and I followed him out leaving a tenner for the tab and wishing Veronica goodbye, to which she just grunted in reply. Kids. What are they like?

Thirty-three

OUTSIDE AS PROMISED was a dark blue automatic Mondeo just old enough to be ready for its first MOT. Ricky held out his hand, keys swinging on a silver key ring. 'Very good,' I said. 'You're better than Hertz.'

'And you get to keep it as long as you want.'

'Well, until it gets too hot anyway.'

He grinned. 'Drive her in good health, Mr S,' he said. 'Anything else you need?'

'Got any speed?' I asked. 'I might need to stay up past my bedtime.'

'Ever known me without?' he asked, and slid a prescription bottle out of the top pocket of his shirt and tossed it to me. 'Ten of the best,' he said.

'How much?'

He put on a pained expression. 'Gratis,' he said. 'I feel bad enough taking your money as it is. This one was too easy. In fact –' he reached again into his pocket and came out with a little silver paper wrap, '– there's something else for you.'

'What?' I asked suspiciously.

'Something from mother nature's larder.'

'Oh yeah.'

'Yeah. Just stick it in your pipe and smoke it. Guaranteed satisfaction every time.'

'Cheers, Ricky,' I said, taking it from him and stashing it in the pocket of my jeans. 'You're alright.'

'Anything for a good customer. Now take it easy and I'll see you soon.'

'You will. Give my love to Veronica.'

'Sure. I think she liked you.'

'You could've fooled me,' I said, and slid into the leather interior of the motor, switched on and listened as the engine purred into life. They must've given it a pre-MOT service at the garage I thought, and waved goodbye to Ricky. He went back inside to his inamorata as I put the gear stick into DRIVE and pulled away from the kerb.

I steered the car carefully through the throng, being careful not to run over any of the punters on the street as I didn't want to be explaining myself and where the car had come from to the local boys in blue, and drove back home with only one spot of bother. As I went through Clapham a police car with headlamps and blue lights flashing and siren screaming came up fast behind me. Damn you, Ricky, I thought as I wondered whether to take off fast, you've done me up you little bastard. But it wasn't to be. The police car swerved round me and was next seen pulled up in front of a new VW Golf driven by a young black man. Things never change, and I'd've been willing to bet his driving licence, insurance and tax were in perfect order. I slid past the two vehicles and made the rest of the journey without a mishap.

Once back I hid the Mondeo in my garage, went inside the house and warmed up a ready-made chop suey in the microwave, but couldn't finish it – I was too on edge.

The last thing I did was phone Finbarr at home. 'How's it going?' I asked when he answered.

'OK. What's the problem?'

'No problem. I was just wondering what you were doing this weekend.'

'Why?'

'No reason. Thought we might get together.'

'No. I'm busy. Sorry.'

'Going away?'

'No. Just staying here.'

'How's Betty?'

'She's good.'

'Why don't we all meet for lunch? Her and the family.'

'No can do. She's off with the kids to her mother's down by the seaside.'

'You didn't fancy going?'

'Listen, Nick. What's all this about? You don't usually worry about my domestic arrangements.' He sounded a bit on edge, and with his holiday plans I wasn't a bit surprised. So it seemed like it was all still on.

'Nothing,' I replied. 'Fancy a drink tomorrow then, if you're on your own?'

'No. I can't. I've got things to do.'

I was gripping the receiver so hard my fist was going white and I couldn't resist saying. 'A little bit of business?'

'Yeah.'

'Well I hope it goes well for you, Fin.'

'Thanks, Nick, me too. Listen, catch up with me after the holiday, yeah? We'll have that drink then.'

'OK, mate,' I said. 'I'll do that.'

And on that friendly note we hung up.

Thirty-four

THE NEXT MORNING dawned brightly, like a firework bursting in the east, the sun climbing across the pale blue, almost white sky around six a.m. I was awake long before that, staring through the window into a night that had hardly seemed to get dark, just dimmed the previous boiling summer's day to give us some respite from the heat.

I hadn't got to sleep until late, or early, depending on how you looked at it. When I'd almost given up, I remembered Ricky's parting gift and dug into my jeans and found the wrap. Inside was a nugget of black, oily opium. Shit, I thought, it's been years. I dug out my old hash pipe and dropped in the dope, lit it with my lighter and inhaled.

It hit me like a runaway train. So hard that I had to sit down fast before I fell down. That's the stuff, I said, as I closed my eyes and drifted off.

And I dreamt about Sheila again. This dream was even more graphic and frightening than the last. I was in an old flat of mine where the back door looked out over a small patio garden with a clothes line that stretched from fence to fence. In the dream there was washing hanging on the line. I was looking out through the window when Sheila pushed through the clothes. She was naked and the bleeding wounds I'd seen when I'd found her in her flat stood out in relief on the white of her skin. I watched as she came closer. I opened the door and she came into my arms as a fierce rain fell from the sky soaking the washing. I held her tightly and started to cry, the tears pouring from my eyes like the rain outside. She said that she was hurting and I tried to comfort her, but could hardly speak for the sobs tearing my chest. My tears washed the gore from her wounds until the cuts were white and bloodless. She kept asking me why she'd had to die, and I could come up with no feasible answer. And then she told me to be careful, to trust no one.

I woke with a terrible start, the sheet that was all that was covering me wrapped around my legs. The bed was soaked with sweat and I'd been crying in my sleep again. I lay there breathless before wiping the dampness from my face, and shivered as the bedclothes cooled.

When the sun's rays moved far enough around the room to reach my face I got up, showered, shaved and made tea. I was too hyper to eat. I looked out of my window. Nothing moved but an old feral cat who loped across the road and disappeared behind the dustbins at the front of the house.

When I'd finished my sparse breakfast, I cleaned my guns and reloaded the magazine of the .22 with ten fresh rounds. For the Detonics I decided to use extended, nine shot clips. I figured I was going to need every bullet I could carry. I filled one and a spare with brass jacketed, hollow point shells, smacked it into the butt, worked the action, popping a bullet into the breech, then dropped out the magazine and put another in its place, locking the hammer back. Now I was ready to rock and roll.

Then I got dressed in jeans, a hooded black long-sleeved sweatshirt, despite the weather. Over the shirt I wore the webbing shoulder holster for the .22 and put on a black cotton Harrington jacket to hide it and the .45 automatic stuck down the back of my pants.

About my person I stashed a mini Maglite torch, a pair of black, skintight leather gloves, sunglasses, the tube of speed that Ricky had given me minus one pill that I dry swallowed, the spare clip for the Detonics, my mobile, and round my neck on a leather bootlace, a Wilkinson Sword FS fighting knife with a metal handle in a leather scabbard.

All the better to stab you with, my dear, I thought.

I didn't want to leave too early, and the morning seemed to take an eternity to pass, with me pacing the floor and chain smoking. But finally the clock on the wall pointed to eleven-thirty and it was time to go.

I went downstairs, put on the sunglasses and gloves, and climbed into the driver's seat of the Mondeo. It was hot inside from the sun and the sweat broke out all over my body and reminded me of the dream I'd had. I switched on the engine and turned the air conditioning up high.

It took me less than thirty minutes to get to Bromley. Finbarr's street was empty, sweltering under the blind yellow eye of the noonday sun that looked down on all our crimes and misdemeanours with an indifferent jaundice that judged them all equally unimportant.

The house was set back in its own grounds surrounded by a high brick wall where dusty ivy hung as if it hadn't the strength to climb further in the heat. The black metal gate at the front was closed as I drove up and stopped the Ford where I could look down the drive to the house. It was large and white and reflected the sun's light so that I might have been in Spain instead of a south London suburb. The double front doors were made of blackened wood gripped with iron hinges and stood at the top of three shallow stone steps. There was no sign of life and I prayed that Fin hadn't been called away by his little firm. I got out of the car and tried the gates. They were locked tight.

I got back into the driver's seat and punched his number into my mobile. The speed was kicking in nicely and I chewed on the inside of my mouth as I waited for the call to connect. He answered quickly. 'Yes,' he said.

'Fancy that drink now, Fin?' I asked.

'Who's this?'

'Nick. Nick Sharman.'

'Listen, Nick,' he said, with exasperation in his voice, 'I haven't got time for a drink. I told you that yesterday. I'm busy. I've got no time.'

'Make time. I thought you had at least until Tuesday morning. Isn't that the plan?'

The exasperation was replaced by suspicion. 'What do you mean?'

'Not on a mobile, Fin,' I said. 'Who knows who might be listening?'

'Where are you, Nick?' he demanded.

'Just outside.'

'What are you doing there?'

'Waiting for you.'

'Why?'

'Unfinished business, Fin.'

'We have no business,' he said.

'Oh yes we do.'

'Like what?'

'Like who killed Sheila.'

'What?'

'Don't play the innocent with me, Fin,' I said, the sweat beginning to run down my body despite Mr Ford's best attempts at air conditioning.

'I don't know what you're talking about.'

'Liar. You bloody liar. Was it you or that fucker Tufnell? Or Morris. Maybe it was him, yeah?'

'I don't know who you're talking about.'

'Don't keep lying, Fin. It's all up. I know everything.'

'You know nothing.'

'We'll see. So are you going to come out and see me or do I have to come in and get you?'

'Nick. It's hot and you've had a bad time. I understand that, so I suggest you turn around and go away again before I call the police.'

'Police. What larks,' I said. 'Now I would've thought they were the last people you'd've wanted to see. This weekend of all weekends.'

'I don't know what you mean.'

'I think you do,' I said.

'Nick. For the last time, go away. And we'll say no more about this silliness.' And he cut me off.

I let the Mondeo drift right up to the gates and sounded the horn. Nothing. I sounded the horn again, and saw Finbarr's anxious face at one of the side windows next to the front doors. The front gates didn't move.

Time to get physical, I thought.

I reversed the car across the wide street, slipped the stick into neutral and wound up the engine until the rev counter redlined and the entire car shook like a bitch on heat. I gripped the wheel with my right hand and shoved the stick into DRIVE with my left. The back wheels spun with a scream of protesting rubber, caught, fishtailed left then right until they found traction and propelled the car forward into the gates, which burst open from the impact. The motor slewed as the surface changed from tarmac to crushed stone. I adjusted the steering and kept my foot on the gas as the Ford roared up the drive, spewing gravel from under its wheels. It hit the concrete steps, which blew out at least one of the front tyres, but the momentum propelled the car forward, up the steps and through the heavy front doors like they were matchwood, and into the hall where I saw Fin's look of surprise as he threw himself out of the way.

I stamped on the brakes and the car broadsided over the polished floor and hit the inside wall on the passenger side with a bang that shook the entire house and dislodged plaster dust from the ceiling.

I was out of the driver's door before the car was still, tugging the Detonics from inside my belt. Fin was holding a gun, but he carried it like an amateur. I slapped it out of his hand and it bounced across the floor. I grabbed the shocked solicitor by the hair, threw him across the hot bonnet of the Mondeo and stuck my gun in his ear. 'Right, you son of a bitch,' I said. 'Will you talk to me now?'

'Calm down,' he said through clenched teeth. 'Don't shoot.'

'Tell me the truth then.'

'I don't know what you're talking about.'

I pulled his hair hard and he screamed like a girl. 'Yes you do.'

'No.'

'Yes.'

'Will you let me up?'

I stood back and allowed him to stand upright, but kept the .45 pointed at his head. He looked round the wreckage of his hall and shook his head, which was dusted with white powder. I had to give it to the man, he was cool. 'Shit,' he said. 'This is going to cost a packet to fix.'

'Then don't add the price of cleaning your brains off the wall,' I said.

'Nick,' he said in a pleading voice. 'I think you've got things all wrong.'

'Don't tell me you've called it off and I've gone to all this trouble for nothing.'

'Called all what off?'

'There you go again, Fin. I really am losing my patience now,' and I ground the barrel of the gun into the soft folds of flesh under his chin. 'Don't fuck with me. I will kill you. That's a promise.'

He must've heard the determination in my voice, or maybe the look on my face convinced him that it was show and tell time and that I wasn't going to go away until I had the truth. 'OK, Nick,' he said, in a placating way. 'You win. What do you want? Part of the action? OK it's yours.'

'Don't fucking insult me, you cunt,' and it took all my willpower not to slap him round the head with the gun in my hand.

'If you don't want money, what do you want?'

'Can't you guess?'

He shook his head.

I went and picked up the gun he'd been holding. It was a snubby nosed .38 five shot revolver. I opened the cylinder and all the chambers were full. The more the merrier I thought as I added the gun to my arsenal.

'You're trying my patience, Fin. Let's go,' I said.

'Where?'

'The City of London mate,' I said. 'Where it's all happening.'

'And what do you intend to do there?'

'Find out who killed Sheila.'

'What?'

'Don't start all that again.'

'It wasn't any of us.'

'Course not.'

'I swear.'

'And I'm supposed to believe you?'

'You must.'

'There's no must about it.'

'Please, Nick, you'll ruin everything. All the months of planning and hard work.'

'Too bad,' I said. 'We'll have to take your car. You can leave mine for the cleaners.'

Thirty-five

FINBARR'S JAGUAR WAS parked in the double garage next to the house. We got to it by a door in the kitchen. I hustled him into the driver's seat through the passenger door, me following, my gun stuck in his kidneys. When we were all sitting comfortably, 'Drive, she said,' I said.

'What?'

'Nothing. A film. Let's get going before one of your neighbours calls the police.'

He started the motor, opened the garage door with a gizmo mounted on the dashboard and drove into the light. He steered the car down the drive and between the wrecked gates. He shook his head as he saw them twisted and buckled and the junction box on the gatepost sparking and fizzing. 'Do you know how much they cost me?' he asked.

'I couldn't even begin to imagine.'

'A fuck of a lot.'

'You're insured,' I said. 'Aren't you?' But I didn't think he was going to live to collect, although I didn't mention it.

He nodded.

'And if that's the worst that happens to you today, I'd count myself lucky.'

He didn't make any comment about that remark.

'Turn left,' I said.

'Where are we going?'

'You know where we're going, Fin,' I told him. 'To wherever your boys are looting and pillaging.'

'I really think you've got it all wrong, Nick,' he protested. 'And you realise you're guilty of kidnap.'

I stuck the Detonics hard into the side of his thigh. 'Kidnapping,' I repeated. 'That's nothing to what you or

Johnny or one of your little crew are guilty of. One of you is a stone killer. One of you killed Sheila.'

'No,' he said. 'It didn't happen like that. I told you, Sheila was a friend. And Johnny was terribly cut up about it.'

'Cut up,' I said coldly. 'Is that a fucking joke or what, you cunt?' I felt my finger tightening on the trigger and I nearly blew the whole deal, and him with it, away.

'No, Nick, please,' he protested when he saw the way things were going. 'I didn't mean it like that. I'm sorry.'

'You will be. Anyway I thought you hadn't seen Johnny for months. Come on, Fin, get your story straight. Make up your mind.'

'I spoke to him,' he stuttered.

'You picked him up on cable? Good show was it?'

'Nick. Tell me, what is all this about?'

'This is all about a roundabout, Fin. It's all about why you meet me in your house with a gun. Hardly the most satisfactory solicitor-client relationship wouldn't you say?'

'You smashed your way onto my property. You did thousands of pounds' worth of damage. This will end up in court.'

I had to laugh and I jabbed the gun harder into his flesh. 'You better hope it does, Fin. But I've got a feeling it won't get that far. You see, Sheila found out about your plan. Whether in the office, or from Johnny or whatever. I don't know. She gave me a letter. You know the kind of thing, "Only to be opened in the event of my death". Well she died, didn't she, Fin, and whoever killed her went through her place and then they went through mine, but they didn't find it. It was too well hidden. And I opened it and she'd written everything she'd found out down. And she'd made a tape at your office of you and your pals Johnny Tufnell and Morris making a plan.'

His face was a picture. 'A tape,' he said. 'Well, I'll be damned . . .'

'Probably,' I said. 'A plan about robbing a safe depository this very weekend. The weekend you're too busy to go out for a drink, and you've got rid of the wife and kids. All very convenient. So don't keep lying to me or I'll kill you now. I know where your little firm is and what they're doing right this minute and I'm going to go down into the sewers and find them and fuck them up and you with them.'

He didn't say a word in reply but I could see that his hands were white on the wheel.

'She was scared that someone might kill her because of what she knew, and that letter was her legacy to me,' I went on after a moment. 'She didn't have much else. A few clothes, some furniture, some junk jewellery and a mortgage. Not much to show for a life was it? Oh, and she had me. Lucky girl. And I wasn't much either. I wasn't there to help her that day. I let her die. It was my fault and I have to live with that. And you, Fin. You were one of the few people who knew she'd be alone that night. 'Cos she worked for you and she was doing overtime and she told you I wouldn't be around. So you, or Johnny, or Morris, or some-fucking-body took advantage of that knowledge and got that knife and killed her. And I think they enjoyed it. I found her don't forget, and I saw what they'd done to her first hand. And you had the balls to go to her funeral and cry crocodile tears all over the coffin. You fucker. Now this gun is loaded, and I do have one in the chamber, and it's a hot load .45, and if I pull the trigger the chances are that it'll blow your fucking leg off, you piece of shit. And you'll go into shock and die. Or maybe you'll just die of blood loss. I don't care either way. And I'll do it, I promise. You don't know what I'm capable of, Fin. Nor do I. But I do know that I've seen so many bad things and done so many bad things that one more won't matter. So you'd better get your shit together and tell me what I want to know. Because otherwise I will hurt you, Fin. Take my word for it. You're in a bad place and it can only get worse.'

'OK,' he said. 'I'll tell you. Just take the gun away.'

I did as he said, only adding, 'And don't be clever, Fin.

Drive real carefully. Obey the highway code and the
traffic laws. And don't flash your lights or otherwise
draw attention to this car or else I'll kill you and take
my chances. Understood?'

He nodded.

'So tell me,' I said.

And he did.

Thirty-six

'YOU THINK YOU'RE pretty smart, don't you?' said Fin as we headed for central London through light traffic.

'Smart,' I rejoindered. 'Just the opposite. Everything was given me on a plate. And believe me I wish I'd never heard about any of it. If Sheila was still alive I wouldn't've. And I'd be a very happy man.'

'Really?'

'Really.'

'So you know everything.'

'I don't know. That's why you're here.'

'So what do you want to know?'

'Anything I left out.'

'There's not much.'

'Always the slimy little lawyer, aren't you?' I said. 'Even with a gun up your backside.' I nudged him with the point of the pistol. 'Humour me, Fin. Tell me true. Start at the beginning, go on to the end, and then stop.'

He nodded. 'OK,' he said, and he was sweating too, even though the Jag's air conditioning was on full blast and it was far superior to the Ford's. 'You're right, there is a bank depository in the City,' he said. 'You know the kind of thing. Private boxes for storing valuables. Johnny Tufnell met a bloke who'd worked there as a security guard. An Australian, name of Morris like you said. Mid-forties. Been around. He'd served in the Australian army in Vietnam when he was very young. Had a bad time of it apparently. He was what they called a tunnel rat. Around Saigon at the end of the war there were miles of them. Tunnels that is. The Viet Cong lived in them and popped up from time to time to do a lot of damage. They sent these kids in with a gun and grenades and high explosive to clear them out. That's where he learnt to lay charges. Morris doesn't like to talk about it but I gather it was rough. Anyway, he worked for the depository for a while last year and got hold of a load of blueprints of the building. They have a vault underground. They're very proud of it. Two foot reinforced concrete walls, a door that weighs a couple of tons. You know the deal. Anyway, the door's on a time lock. No one can get in this weekend from late Friday until Tuesday morning after the holiday. And Morris discovered its one weakness. The vaults that is. It's built onto the original floor of the building. And the building itself is over a hundred years old. The floor is only about six inches thick. The foundations are solid, but the floor is weak. And then he did some more research. Underneath the city it's like a honeycomb. Sewers, conduits, tunnels. He got plans of the area and reckoned that with a little work he could dig a tunnel from a disused sewer outlet bang up underneath the vault. Then using high explosive he could blow the floor and get in. And with high powered drilling equipment he could open the boxes. He reckoned there were a thousand of them and most of them were packed with goodies.'

'Yeah,' I said. So far it was exactly as I'd heard it on the tape. No surprises, thank God.

'Yeah. Cash. Tax skims. Jewels, dope. You name it and it was down there. If each box only contained a grand that was a cool million. And he told us that he'd seen boxes that contained that much alone.'

'So where did you come in? Why did he pick on you?'

'The job took planning. Time. And they had to go carefully. More time. So they needed wages. And then there was equipment. High explosive, weapons and of course the drilling equipment once they got inside. Johnny Tufnell picked me. He knew I had the wherewithal.'

'You helped Johnny before.'

'Occasionally.'

'You've bankrolled jobs for him.'

'A few.'

'Running with the hare and the hounds, eh Fin. That can be dangerous you know.'

'I know.'

'So how many are down there now?' I asked.

'Four. Johnny Tufnell, Morris and two others.'

'A right ambitious little firm. Have these other two got names?'

'One's Grady. Muscle. A friend of Johnny's from when he was inside. A dangerous man by all accounts. I haven't met him. The further I kept away the better as far as I was concerned. And the other . . . I don't know. Dobson, Robson, something like that.'

'And that's it. No surprises, Fin.' I jabbed him with the gun again.

'No. I swear. Four was fine. That's all the job needed. Why split the take any more ways? And the more that knew about it the more chance that someone would find out . . .' He looked over at me.

'So you should've been more careful where you talked about it.'

'I can't believe Sheila did that to me.'

'It was nothing to do with you. She did it in case your pal Johnny came round to her place and started up where he left off. Giving her grief. Knocking her about. She didn't give a shit about the job itself. She wasn't going to grass you up. Unless she had to.'

'And you think one of us killed her?'

'Who else?'

He was silent.

'So what about the alarms on the building, Fin?' I asked. 'Isn't the place belled up?' Although I knew, I wanted to keep him talking. Give him no time to think.

'Sure. Morris explained that. There are motion sensors that set off bells and whistles and a silent alarm to the local nick. But so what? They blow the floor. Not a big hole. Just big enough to get in and out with the gear and the alarm goes off. Maybe lots of alarms all round the area. Who knows? Who cares? In fact the more the merrier. Confuse the issue. The coppers call out the keyholder who comes down and sees that everything is secure on the outside of the vault. But he can't get inside. Not until Tuesday morning. So he resets the alarm and goes back home. There's nothing else he can do. Old Bill have to put it down to an earth tremor or something.'

'But what happens if they smell a rat and go underground themselves?' A tunnel rat I thought, but didn't vocalise it. This was no time for jokes.

'I told you the place is like a maze. There's a thousand places down there. Miles of tunnels. They could search for a month and never find any trace of digging. Morris has been down there and sussed it out. I think he feels at home underground.'

If he gets in my way he'll be there permanently I thought. And you too, you little bastard.

Thirty-seven

FINBARR DROVE OVER London Bridge and into the City which surprisingly was quite busy, it being a Sunday, and a holiday Sunday at that. It was mostly tourists on foot, fat Yanks in bad clothes gawping at buildings that were old before their country was colonised, dragging spoilt kids round the sights, when all they really wanted to see was their next Big Mac and fries. But that was good as far as I was concerned. The more people wandering about the better. At least Finbarr and I wouldn't be so conspicuous. It was quiet in the car after Finbarr's confession, or part confession at least. He still hadn't owned up to the most important part – Sheila's murder, so I put on the radio. It was tuned to one of London's soft rock stations, Liberty or Heart FM, I didn't know which, they all sounded the same to me. Non-stop Celine Dion, Whitney Houston or the Corrs – crap one and all. At the end of the record came the news and weather. The hot spell was about to break we were told, and heavy thunderstorms were heading our way from Spain. Big deal. I had more important things to think about.

Then we hit the ring of steel. There were two cars in front of us going through a section of the road that had been coned off, and it was being guarded by one bored looking uniformed WPC who gestured for us to pull over. Just my sodding luck! Finbarr looked terrified as I slid the gun out of sight between the seats and hit the OFF button on the stereo. 'Make it convincing, Fin,' I said. 'Or I might just shoot you and take my chances.'

'What about her?' he hissed, as the female officer walked round the car.

'Her too,' I said, but that was just to scare him into being good. There was no way I was going to shoot at some poor innocent woman copper just because she happened to be in the right place at the wrong time. Or the wrong place at the right time. I never could work that one out. But he wasn't to know that. Or at least I hoped he wasn't.

'I might just tell her you've got a gun,' he said.

'And I might just tell her why,' I replied. 'That's going to fuck your boys up big time. This way you've still got a chance.'

He let down the electric window on his side and the WPC peered in. 'Where are you going, gentlemen?' she asked.

I saw Finbarr's Adam's apple going as he swallowed. 'I'm just dropping my friend off at Liverpool Street Station,' he said raspily.

I smiled at the copper across him. She smiled back. I'd still got it.

'Off on holiday?' she said to me.

'No,' I replied. 'Just been visiting. Got to get back to the kids for bank holiday.'

'Whereabouts?'

'Colchester,' I said. It was the only place I could think of that I knew was reached from Liverpool Street.

'Lucky you,' she said. 'I'm working all weekend. And in this heat too.'

'Someone's got to keep the streets safe,' I said.

'That's right. I'm an Essex girl myself. A little village just outside Colchester as a matter of fact.'

'Best people in the world,' I said through gritted teeth. Just my bloody luck again. If she started comparing favourite pubs then I was done for.

'True. Anyway, I won't keep you. Have a good journey.' And she waved us on.

Finbarr put the car back into gear and drove off. 'Well done, Fin,' I said. 'Oscar-winning performance.'

'I hope my boys shoot you,' he said.

'You've said that before.'

'No. I said they might shoot you. Now I want them to.'

'Don't push your luck, son,' I said. 'Don't forget who you're talking to.'

He gave me a dirty look but said nothing more.

'So where do we go now?' I asked.

'There's an NCP at the back of London Wall in Fore Street,' said Finbarr. 'It's open all weekend. I'll drop the car there, then we walk.'

The car park was small, almost empty, and fully automatic, with no attendant in the kiosk. Finbarr put the car into an empty space on the ground floor and we went into the street. I put my gun into the pocket of my jacket but reminded him that my finger was on the trigger.

'I'm not likely to forget,' he said.

We walked to the corner of Moor Lane and across the road into Union Street to an old-fashioned building where Finbarr stopped and took a set of keys from his pocket. On the way I flipped up the hood of my sweatshirt and covered my face with my hand. I didn't want the cameras to see me clearly. 'What's this then?' I asked, grabbing his arm before he could get the key in the lock.

'The way in.'

'I thought that was a manhole cover down the road.'

'Use your loaf, Nick,' he said. 'We couldn't be going in and out of that all the time. Somebody would've sussed us for sure. That was just for Morris's recon. When he was sure it would work we needed a proper base of operations. Somewhere with some room to move, and this is where I rented an office and some storage space as a front.'

'OK, I believe you,' I said. 'Just one thing. Are there going to be any surprises inside? Like one of your boys waiting?'

He shrugged. 'Not yet. They'll still be in the depository, or should be, opening the boxes. They're due to start shifting the gear after midnight.'

I watched as he opened the street door and we went inside, where a large, mosaic floored entrance hall stood empty. As we crossed the threshold a buzzer erupted into life and he went to a keypad and punched in six numbers which killed the sound. 'No security outside of office hours,' he explained. 'No nosy guards around, which made it perfect for us. I've got an office at the back, and a storeroom in the basement.'

'And a route into the sewers,' I said.

He nodded.

'Let's take a look then, Fin,' I said, taking the Detonics out from its hiding place. 'You lead the way. Just keep quiet in case there's been a change of plan.'

We walked across the hallway, past the deserted reception desk and through a set of double doors into a long, wide hallway with doors on both sides, each with its little brass or plastic plate informing us of the firms that resided inside. 'Which one's yours?' I asked.

'This one,' he replied. The plate on the door read: INDEPENDENT REMOVALS.

'A sense of humour,' I remarked. 'What's inside?'

'A desk and a phone,' he said.

'Show.'

He used another key on the ring to unlock the door. I pushed him aside and opened it gently, pistol first. He'd been telling the truth. 'Go on then,' I said, and he led me through another set of doors into a narrower hall without carpet and finally to a door marked FIRE EXIT. He pushed the bar and we were on the fire stairs, then we headed down one flight to the basement to another fire door. Finbarr shoved it open and fumbled for a light switch that turned on fluorescent tubes which illuminated a bare-walled corridor lined with yet more doors. At the end of the corridor, set flush into the floor was a square manhole cover.

He stood over it and said, 'This is it.'

'Come on then,' I said.

'A minute.' And he unlocked one of the doors to expose a darkened room. He hit the lights again and I saw that the room contained a motley collection of equipment including a huge pile of cardboard boxes, a couple of torches that made the tiny Maglite I'd brought with me look as powerful as a candle, and a pair of brightly painted tools that I didn't immediately recognise. In the far corner was a pile of clothes, iced brown with mud, on top of a coil of rope.

He picked up one of the tools, hooked the end into one of the grooves in the cover and with a tug pulled it out of the floor. The bad boys had obviously thought of everything.

'Stop there,' I said, and looked into the hole that the cover had filled. It was very dark inside and a bad smell hit my nostrils.

'This leads into the main sewer,' he explained. 'It's a bit of a walk to where we're going. But it was the closest place we could get that led directly to the depository and had no night watchman.'

'So what's the exact plan?' I said.

'Simple. Right now the chaps are looting the boxes. Early tomorrow morning they start transferring the stuff through the tunnels to here, where they'll store it in that room.' He pointed to the open door beside me. 'Then they box it up in the cartons provided, and on Tuesday morning early we bring round a truck and load it up. Simple. With any luck we'd've been over the river before the time lock on the vault tripped.'

'And Independent Removals are out of business.'

'Exactly.'

'Nice idea, Fin. Pity it ain't going to work.'

'Don't be so sure, Nick. Those boys are bad people. They don't take prisoners. If you're not careful they'll leave you down there to rot with the rest of the sewage.'

'Maybe they'll be doing me a favour,' I said, picking up the rope and hanging it round my neck. 'Come on, let's take a walk.'

Thirty-eight

I LET FINBARR go down first. It was a dangerous thing to do but I had no choice under the circumstances, so I gave him one of the big torches, kept my gun in my hand and warned him that if he tried to make a run for it I'd have no alternative but to shoot. Of course if he'd thought about it he'd've realised that I didn't know where the hell we were going, and if he managed to vanish into the labyrinth below I'd be literally up shit creek without a paddle. And the odour from beneath told me exactly what shit creek smelled like. Man, but it was strong. The long dry spell had ripened the contents of the sewer until it was hard to breathe without dry-retching, but I just swallowed the bile and kept going.

I followed him down the narrow, rusty, wobbly ladder that led into the sewer, one handed, holding my pistol in the other with the other big torch stuck in my belt and relying on his for light. Once again, if he'd thought about it he could've just killed his light and left me halfway up the ladder with my thumb up my arse whilst he made his escape. Thank Christ it was only a short drop because the ladder felt as if it was going to give way with every step. It must have been as old as the sewer system and no one had bothered to maintain it over its long life. When I finally got to the bottom he was waiting like a good dog. I didn't give him a pat on the head. The sewer was indeed ancient. Christ knows how long it had been since a bunch of navigators, as they had been called, dug through the soil under the city and built this vaulted brick tunnel where we found ourselves. The beam from Finbarr's torch illuminated the stained brickwork that hung with stalactites of green moss that dripped into the slow moving river of filth that moved beside the narrow walkway where we stood. I took the other torch from my belt and added its light to his.

'Which way?' I asked, breathing through my mouth against the stink, and my voice echoed as if we were in a cathedral.

'This way,' he said, and moved off to our right. 'But watch out for rats, they can get quite proprietorial.'

The only rat I could see was Finbarr himself but I didn't say it. Instead I stopped him with a word. 'Wait,' I said. 'How far is it?' It had suddenly occurred to me that I might be walking into a trap, what with all the light and conversation we were having. There could easily be someone waiting just around the corner with a gun.

'Not too far,' he replied. 'About ten, fifteen minutes walk.'

'OK,' I said. 'You lead the way, but keep your voice down. I don't want anyone to hear us coming.'

'Fine,' he said. I didn't like it one bit. I had no choice but to follow him, and moved off behind Finbarr, our shadows dancing together against the walls as we went. 'Stop,' I ordered after we'd gone a few yards. 'How do I find my way back?'

'I'll show you,' said Fin, but by the look in his dark eyes that reflected the torch light back at me, we both knew only one of us would make the return trip. If that.

We followed the sewer for perhaps three quarters of a mile, then came to a junction and took a right turn. The walkway became narrower and the roof lower and the smell stronger if that were possible, and the brickwork beneath our feet more slippery as we moved into what seemed to be an even older part of the sewer. All along our route someone had marked X's in chalk at about shoulder height, and Finbarr pointed them out to me. 'That's for us,' he said. 'It's not far now.'

'Good,' I replied.

Then there was another right and the ceiling became even lower. Set into the wall was an iron door that looked as if it hadn't been opened for a hundred years. 'This is it,' he said.

'Fine.'

'So what now?' he asked.

'I'm going to tie you up and leave you here, then I'll go in and find your buddies. And if it turns out that you've lied to me, I'll come back and kill you.'

'They're in there.'

'Four, right?'

'Right.'

'Come on then,' and I pulled the coil of rope over my head. The pistol wavered in my hand and without warning Finbarr threw the torch he was carrying at me. I ducked as it smashed into the brickwork beside me and bounced once on the walkway before falling into the sludgy river next to us where it floated on the surface, as he took off. I shouted for him to stop, but he ignored me. I fired once, twice, the muzzle flashes bright in the semi-darkness and the sound exploding off the walls so loudly that they almost split my eardrums. The first bullet missed by a mile and struck sparks off the walls so I took more care with the second, which hit him in the middle of his back and threw him into the water where he floated face down, perfectly still, just another piece of shit amongst so many others, as the torch he'd thrown was sucked down into the mire.

I shone the torch I was carrying onto his body and watched as it bobbed along with the slow flow of effluence, dropped the rope that I didn't need, then I turned and opened the door that he'd shown me. I briefly pointed my light down and saw that inside there were fresh tracks in the dirt that lay on the floor of the tunnel, and I deduced that Fin had brought me to the right place. Shit, I thought as I turned off my torch and hoisted myself into the darkness. Here goes nothing.

Out of the blue and into the black. That's what the tunnel rats in Vietnam had called going into the maze of shafts that Victor Charlie had built underground. I don't know

where that came from. It must've been from some book
I'd read or film I'd seen.

And it was black inside that tunnel, the kind of blackness
you rarely see in our industrial society, where lights burn
night and day.

Out of the blue into the black, maybe never to return.

But that was the chance I had to take, and I slid the
warm gun that had killed Finbarr into my jeans at the
back, took my knife from its scabbard around my neck
and clenched it between my teeth pirate fashion.

This is for you, Sheila, I thought as I squeezed into the
narrow tube and pulled the door closed behind me.

Thirty-nine

I HATED IT inside that pitch black tube, not knowing how far I'd have to crawl and what or who I might meet. The rough ceiling scraped my head and back and the dirt underneath my gloves and knees was damp and sticky. And it stank too, like there was a million years of shit all around me, which there probably was going right back from when a bunch of cavemen first set up camp next to the river that blocked their way to the south and the sea beyond.

I've never liked enclosed spaces ever since I was a kid, and this was the worst I'd ever experienced.

I allowed myself one quick burst from the torch after half a minute or so, but all it revealed was more tunnel and thick blackness ahead where the light ran out. And it was getting warmer, like this was the entrance to hell and the devil was waiting just down the road apiece to welcome me to eternal fire and damnation.

Not that I didn't deserve it.

Then it occurred to me that Fin had been lying, that he'd shown me some other tunnel that led nowhere, and panic hit hard. It took me all my willpower not to start back the way I'd come, but I managed to calm myself and I lay flat and tried to hug the ground as the roof of the pipe seemed to come down on me, and I swore I could feel the weight of earth and clay and the buildings above and that they were all ready to come crashing down on me and squash me like a bug.

After what I reckoned to be another half minute, which could have been five seconds or two hours, I switched on the torch for a second again. Same sight, same feeling of claustrophobia. How those boys in Vietnam had done this sort of gig day after day I couldn't imagine. And it was getting hotter and the sweat was stinging my eyes like acid.

And then, all of a sudden I felt a change in the atmosphere as if a weight had been lifted off me, and I thought the quality of the blackness changed. I gave a third burst on the torch and found that I was in a square dugout with another tunnel leading off at right angles, but this time the tunnel was fresh and it had been shored up with wooden supports.

Fin had brought me to the right place.

And there were heavyweight black garbage bags in the dugout. Piled up in corner. The loot the boys were bringing out, it must be. I checked one. It was full of cash. Currencies from all over the world. Pounds, Dollars, Francs, Marks. A bloody fortune.

And it had got lighter. Definitely. I set off up the fresh tunnel and when it turned I saw some way further up a battery-driven lamp set into the wall. Not much of a light, but a light nevertheless, that told me I was getting close to Tufnell and his crew.

Then I heard a sound, a faint scrape from beyond the dim light. I killed the torch and moved backwards into the dugout, pressed myself into the corner away from the tunnel entrance and waited. It could've been a rat, and I was sure it was. But one of the two legged variety.

And then the light faded as someone passed between it and me. Now who could this be?

I heard him breathing hard and he sounded like he was dragging something behind him. More swag. Which meant at least one of his hands was occupied with whatever he was dragging and the other was pulling him towards me. Perfect. That meant he wasn't carrying any weapons.

I took the knife out of my mouth and held it tightly, feeling the dimples in the metal handle pressing into the flesh of my hand through the thin leather of my gloves, and waited.

Just like whoever had stabbed Sheila had waited outside her door for her to answer it.

Come to Daddy, I whispered to myself, and there he was. A dark shape against the darker whole. I hunkered onto my knees and flashed my torch straight into a face I didn't recognise, and the look of surprise, and the scream that left his lips was perfect. 'Who the fuck—?' he said.

'Your worst nightmare,' I replied as I dropped the torch I was carrying in my left hand and grabbed the sweaty fringe of hair he wore across his forehead and stabbed the knife I was clutching in my right into his throat, and felt the warm surge onto my glove as I pulled out the blade and stabbed again and again, until the only sound in the dugout was my breathing and the drip drip drip of his blood onto the ground.

Forty

WHEN I WAS sure he had stopped breathing I dropped the knife on the ground, wiped my blood-sodden gloves on his clothes and checked him for weapons. He was carrying a small calibre revolver in a holster in the small of his back, which I added to my arsenal, and I thought that Blair's poxy government and the cops had got all handguns off the street. That was a waste of the sodding taxpayer's money if ever I saw one. Then I shone the torch onto his face, or what was left of it. It was like I thought, I didn't know him, even though his mother would hardly recognise him, the state he was in now. And I wasn't likely to be introduced at this late stage in the game. Still, that's life. Then I had a look in the heavy duty, double thick, reinforced garbage bag he'd been dragging behind him. It was full of more cash, some very expensive looking jewellery and a thick sheaf of bearer bonds. Not bad for a couple of days' work, especially combined with what had already been stashed at the front of the tunnel.

I dragged it and him into the dugout and pushed both as far into one corner as I could, then I set off in the direction he'd come from. I put my knife back in its scabbard. I reckoned it was too late for knives now. I just hoped I didn't meet anyone else coming towards me.

I crawled along the tunnel that Tufnell's boys had dug, through a half inch or so of filthy water that had collected on the bottom, past more battery powered lights they had set into the walls that had been strengthened with wood, until it started to head uphill and I could smell the remnants of the charge that had blown out the floor of the vault, and then finally I found where brick and concrete had been blown, and above me was the vault itself.

I took the Detonics from inside the back of my jeans

and popped my head through the hole. Inside the massive vault it was carnage lit by a single, powerful gas lantern that hissed like a snake in a bag.

The blast itself seemed to have been perfectly judged to blow the floor and not much else, but afterwards the chaps had rifled every box in the place and the floor was covered with the empty drawers, money, papers, books, photos, jewellery and all sorts. Personal stuff that meant a lot to the people who'd stored them, but nothing to the thieves.

As I scoped the room I saw the remaining trio of robbers filling more black sacks with loot like three of the seven dwarves. I was surprised they weren't singing 'Whistle While You Work'.

One of them was Johnny Tufnell, who'd put on a little weight since I'd seen him last. The second was a big, powerful bloke, stripped to the waist, his muscular body greased with sweat. The other was an older man, grizzled and grey haired who I imagined had to be Morris, the Australian Vietnam veteran Fin had told me about who'd cooked up the plan to rob the depository, the bloke I'd stabbed having been too young to have taken part in that old, half-forgotten war in South-East Asia.

As I made to climb up into the vault and join them, the barrel of my gun scraped on the concrete and the big fellow turned and said, 'Come on Billy, time's a-wasting, my man.'

At least I knew the name of the man I'd butchered. 'Sorry, my man,' I said. 'Billy's otherwise engaged.'

He looked at me in amazement and dived for a leather jacket that was draped over a pile of empty safe deposit boxes that I assumed held a weapon, and I shot him twice. The twin explosions of the heavy calibre gunshots were deafening in the confined space but he kept going, tugging a pistol from the jacket, so I shot him again. And do you know the fucker wouldn't die. He turned towards me, the gun's barrel pointing in my direction until I put a bullet in his face and he crashed over the pile of boxes and into the wall and lay still. Meanwhile the older bloke had pulled a gun from somewhere on his person and got off a shot that whipped past my head and smacked into the wall behind me. I shot him too, but this time it only took one bullet to put him down. I was improving. Tufnell made a move as well, but I wanted him alive and fired to miss, and after the bullet had finished ricocheting round the room I said, 'Don't do it, Johnny. We've got things to talk about.'

He froze and looked at me through the smoke and the stink of spent gunpowder, and I saw recognition bloom on his face like a flower. 'Nick Sharman,' he said. 'What the fuck are you doing here?'

Forty-one

'JUST VISITING WITH an old pal. Looking for a little chat,' I replied, holding the gun on him whilst I checked out Morris. He was dead with his open eyes staring up at the ceiling. I wondered what he saw. And what he'd thought as I'd come up out of the tunnel, dressed all in black, and shot him. Maybe for a moment he imagined he was back in Vietnam and I was the Vietcong come for him at last. I checked his jacket and found another revolver. I opened the cylinder and let the bullets fall to the floor then tossed it on the ground. I didn't have a pocket free for yet another gun. Then I checked the other bloke. Not that he needed much checking. He'd taken enough lead to kill a horse. He was dead. His gun and bullets joined Morris's in the dirt.

'Are you crazy?' said Tufnell. 'You've killed them. What the fuck did you do that for?'

'Because I could,' I replied.

'You've ruined everything,' he said in disbelief, as if I'd opened the oven door on his Victoria sponge and it had gone all flat.

'Tough.'

'How did you get here?'

'Finbarr brought me. You got a gun?'

He shook his head.

'Put your arms out,' I ordered. He did as he was told and I frisked him from behind. He'd told the truth. 'You never did like guns much did you, Johnny?' I said. 'Prefer knives don't you?'

'Where is Fin?' he asked, ignoring my question.

'Hip deep in shit, son,' I replied as I stepped back and moved round so that I was in front of him and could see his face. 'Just like you.'

'What do you mean?'

I enlightened him. 'Dead,' I said.

'Where?'

'In the main sewer.'

'You killed him?'

I nodded. 'Just like I killed your pal Billy. Now which one of you killed her? Was it you? Or was it him?' I pointed at Morris. 'Or was it big, bad Billy? Or the other fella? Come on Johnny, you can tell me. Or was it Finbarr himself? Tell me, you shit, or I swear I'll kill you too.'

'What are you talking about?' He seemed genuinely ignorant of what I was talking about. But then he'd had lots of practice at coming on all injured innocence in police stations up and down the country.

'Sheila, Johnny,' I said slowly, as if to someone retarded. 'Our mutual *amour*. Who killed her?'

'I don't know.'

I reached inside my sweatshirt and pulled out my blood-stained commando knife and put the needle point on Tufnell's Adam's apple, then I put the Detonics barrel into the centre of his forehead, the gun was still cocked and my finger was hard on the trigger. Just like when I'd put it against my temple back at the house the night that Sheila died. He was only a couple of pounds' pressure from dying and he knew it. 'Don't lie, man,' I said. 'Don't fuck me around or I'll just shoot you out of hand. With all five of you dead I'm sure to have got the right man. Or would you prefer I use the knife on you like I did on good old Billy, like one of you did on Sheila?'

'You're wrong, Sharman. Dead wrong.'

I had to laugh, although even to me it didn't sound like the laugh of a sane man. What the fuck it sounded like to him I have no idea, but he wasn't looking too happy at the sound of it and paled visibly. 'Don't insult my intelligence, Johnny,' I said. 'Don't fucking lie to a liar. It doesn't work.'

'What are you on, Sharman?'

'Not much. A little bit of speed is all. Just enough to keep me sharp, like this knife.' And I laughed again, and Johnny Tufnell, hard man that he was, went even paler.

'Well you're wrong,' he said, and there was a tremor in his voice as he spoke.

'I'm not wrong, Johnny. Even old Bill are looking for you for it. You've been keeping a low profile, brother. Underground as it were. If only they knew eh?'

'Listen man. As God is my witness, I never touched Sheila.'

'That makes a change doesn't it? From what I heard you were always touching her when you were together. Touching her hard. Fisty. And don't bring God into the equation.'

'That was then, man. I hadn't seen her.'

'Since when?'

'Since just after you two started seeing each other.'

'I still don't believe you, John. You see she left me a letter and a tape of you and Morris's first meeting with Finbarr at his office. And whoever killed her was looking for it. They spun her place, then mine.'

'It wasn't me.'

'So was it Fin?'

'Fin? No way. Fin loved that girl. He'd loved her since before I even met her. He was all fucked up when she was killed. I mean it.'

'So it was Billy or Morris or our unnamed friend lying there with four bullets in him?'

'No. Morris knew nothing about Sheila. He'd never even seen her. And Billy was just muscle. So was the other bloke. We just brought them in for the digging.'

'So it must've been you.'

'It wasn't me,' he pleaded. 'Listen. I'll tell you what happened. When she kicked me out I told her that if she hooked up with anyone else, anyone, I'd kill him whoever he was. She didn't. Go out with anyone I mean. Not for months until you came along. Fin told me all about it after we'd had that meeting and I went round one night when you weren't there. I told her I'd meant what I said, and she told me that she knew about this job. I didn't know exactly how much she knew but it was enough. I guessed that me turning up at the office had scared her and she'd been listening in. I didn't know anything about a letter or a tape.'

'So it was very convenient when she died.'

'Oh shit,' he said. 'I never thought about it. Not until later, anyway. Yeah, it was convenient. But Christ, Sharman, I'd never do a thing like that. I'm no killer, I'm a thief.'

'So tell me what happened when you saw her that night?'

'She told me that if anything happened to you, anything, an accident, anything – even if you stubbed your toe getting out of the bath – she'd blow the whistle on this caper. I didn't know she knew anything about it. It stopped me in my tracks I can tell you. We'd invested time and money into the job, and the returns were so huge that I let it go. I swear, man. I didn't tell Finbarr in case he pulled out. I didn't tell Morris either. And the other two were just donkeys. No one knew she knew except me. That's the truth.'

'So it had to be you, stands to reason,' I said. 'You've just convicted yourself out of your own mouth.'

'No,' he almost screamed. 'Listen to me. When I heard she was dead I couldn't believe it. But I loved her too, you know, in my own way, and I promise you I was down here when it all happened. We all were. Even Finbarr was around that morning. I'll never forget it. He was one of the first to hear about it, you know that, and he found out the time of death and told me. We were all underground. The boys would tell you if they could.'

I almost believed him.

'I almost believe you,' I said. 'Except it's the perfect motive. Kill Sheila and she couldn't grass you up.'

'If you stayed well she'd keep her mouth shut. That was

the deal, and Sheila always kept her word. You know that. You must.'

Once again I almost believed him.

'So who killed her, Johnny? Rupert the Bear?'

'I swear I don't know, Sharman.'

'I do,' came a voice from behind us, and when I turned Lucy Madden was standing on the edge of the hole in the floor holding a silenced semi-automatic pistol, and a big, blonde woman dressed in motorcycle leathers was climbing up behind her.

Forty-two

AND SUDDENLY, LIKE the sun coming out after a prolonged period of rain, everything became clear, and I released that once again I'd been taken for a mug. 'You,' I said. 'I don't fucking believe it.'

'Believe it,' she said back.

'I'll be damned.'

She nodded in agreement.

I saw the look in Tufnell's eyes as he clocked Lucy. I imagine it was pretty similar to the expression on mine when I had first seen her outside my front door on the day Sheila had died. 'Like her, isn't she?' I said.

'Jesus, I never knew.'

'You two never met?' She'd told me so many lies by then, I didn't know what to believe.

Tufnell shook his head.

'Then let me introduce you. Johnny Tufnell, this is Lucy. Sheila's sister, and unless I'm much mistaken, the person who stabbed her to death. Some families huh? And the other one must be Georgina, her bull dyke friend. Attractive. If you like brick shit houses. Think what Jerry Springer would make of this little lot.'

'Shut up both of you,' said Lucy, 'and put down the gun and knife, Nick. Gently. Then move away from him and them.'

'But I'm right, aren't I, Luce?' I said. 'It was you all the time.'

'Shut up, Nick, and do as you're told,' said Lucy, and raised her gun.

I did exactly what I was told then, moving away from Johnny Tufnell and laying the Detonics and the commando knife carefully on the floor.

'What the fuck is going on, Sharman?' demanded Tufnell. 'Did you bring her here?'

'Not me, man,' I replied, then to her. 'You've been following me haven't you?'

'You and a trail of bodies,' said Lucy. 'Thanks for doing most of our work for us.'

'I knew it,' I said. 'I knew someone was watching me.'

'We've got no time for this rubbish,' said Lucy. 'Georgie, put the cuffs on them.'

'You think of everything,' I said as the blonde hauled out a number of sets of metal cuffs from the ample bosom of her leather jacket. 'You going to get your tits out for the boys are you, Georgie?' I baited her. 'Give us a feel, there's a girl.'

'Shut up,' she hissed and mistakenly passed between Tufnell and Lucy, which gave him the opportunity to move, kicking the lantern over, extinguishing the flame and plunging us into darkness, which was when it all went on top.

Lucy fired twice, the sound silenced by the suppressor, but in the strobe of the muzzle flash I saw Tufnell fling up his arms as he was hit and fall backwards. Then Lucy pulled the trigger again and the bullet plucked at my jacket and sweatshirt and a ribbon of fire burnt its way across my ribs. I cried out in pain as I dropped to the floor, scrabbling for my gun as I went. I fumbled, almost lost it in the bright memory of the flame on the retinas of my eyes, and found it again more by luck than judgment and clutched it to my chest like a long lost lover.

In the silence that followed the short engagement I heard Georgina say, 'Did you get them?'

'Shut up,' barked Lucy in reply.

And then Georgina did the most stupid thing she could've done under the circumstances. From somewhere on her person she found a Zippo lighter and fired it up. Maybe she was convinced that Johnny and I were both out of the game, or maybe she was scared of the dark, or maybe she was such a rank amateur that she didn't know any better, but I heard the flywheel rasp and like a good

Zippo it caught on the first spark and illuminated her face. I fired straight into it twice and blew what brains she had out of the back of her head. The mechanism of the .45 blew back empty and I rolled away as Lucy returned fire. The bullets whistled round the vault like tiny space ships.

'We're even now,' I said through the ringing in my ears as I pulled the revolver I'd taken off Fin from my pocket. 'One on one.'

Lucy fired at the sound of my voice but I'd already moved and was hunkered down behind Tufnell's body.

'You killed her, you fucker,' she said.

'The killing of Sister George.'

'Bastard.'

'And you killed Sheila,' I reminded her.

'Stupid bitch. She could've been rich.'

'Helping you take the loot from Finbarr and Johnny and their mates.'

'Got it in one, Nick.'

'Did she tell you about all this so that you could nick them?'

'Yes. And get Johnny out of her life once and for all.'

'But you had different ideas.'

'Right again.'

'But why kill her? She was your own flesh and blood for God's sake.'

'She was a bloody fool, always getting mixed up with the wrong men.'

Did she mean me I wondered. 'And you're supposed to be a copper,' I said.

'That's fine coming from you.'

'But you're a high flyer. Why give it all up?'

'Don't be stupid, Nick,' she said, and I knew she was moving round to my left. 'Why should I put up with all the shit I get just for a rotten copper's wages? All the old bollocks my so called colleagues give me, just to be one of the boys.'

'I thought you were one of the boys,' I said.

'Shut up.'

'You're going to have to pay,' I said.

'What lousy film did you get that line from?'

'It's the truth, Lucy. One way or another, I promise you will pay for what you did.'

'Eat this,' and she fired off half a dozen rounds in my general direction, one at least smacking into Tufnell's dead body. Not that he cared.

'I hope you've got plenty of ammunition there, honey,' I said when she stopped firing.

'Enough to deal with you.'

'Well, we've got all the time in the world to find out.'

'Plenty of time, Nick. But unless I'm much mistaken you're bleeding. Bad is it? I hope so. And you're stuck inside and I'm blocking your exit.'

'Stalemate then, darling.'

'We'll see about that won't we.'

Forty-three

'So what do you reckon?' I asked after a bit. 'What is it now? Sunday evening? If we stay around like this long enough, in thirty-six hours or so someone will come along and open the vault and then the game will be up. Pity we didn't bring the Scrabble set to pass the time. Or some sandwiches would be nice. Didn't you get Georgie to make up a picnic?' I shifted as I spoke and felt a liquid pain from my bullet wound. I wondered how serious it was. I didn't fancy dying down here.

'I don't intend to be here that long,' said Lucy in reply. 'I am a police officer after all.'

'What the fuck's that got to do with anything? What are you going to do then? Call for back-up? I don't think your mobile will work this far underground. And even if you could, how are you going to explain this little lot?'

'That you're a murderer and bank robber, and that I caught you and your accomplices in the act. Just as thieves fell out.'

It was almost laughable, and I would've done if my ribs hadn't hurt so much. 'And what about Georgie girl?' I asked. 'Why was she here? To handle first aid?'

'I'll think of something.'

'Oh yeah, and I'm just going to stand for that am I?'

'You might not be around to stand for anything.'

'You've got to catch me first.'

She was silent again for a minute or two. 'Or we could join forces,' she said, with a wheedling tone to her voice. 'There's enough here for both of us. More than enough.'

'And I'm supposed to trust you after all that's happened?'

'That's right.'

'I don't think so, Lucy.'

'Why not?'

'Because you killed your own sister for this. My girl-friend. What makes you think I'd believe you'd web me into it?'

'Trust me.'

'And your girlfriend still warm. Your girlfriend that I killed. I don't think so.'

'Well, I killed your girlfriend so that makes us even.'

What a cold hearted cunt. But that's women for you. 'You're unbelievable,' I said. 'Your girlfriend wasn't my sister. Mine was yours. How the fuck could you do that?'

'We were never that close. I told you that.'

I couldn't find a retort to that one.

'Nick. Believe me,' she went on, 'much as I value human relationships, I value money more.'

'I believe you. I found Sheila's body don't forget.'

'That's in the past. And we had something together didn't we?'

'One drunken fuck. Hardly the basis for a long lasting relationship.'

'But all this money . . .'

'No, Lucy. As far as I'm concerned I'll take the "Stay here till Tuesday" option. I reckon the cops will at least listen to my story.'

'You've killed how many?' she said in reply. 'You're in deep shit, my friend. Do you think you're going to walk away from this little lot with just a slap on the wrist?'

'I'll take my chances.'

'Then of course there's always plan B,' she said.

'Which is?'

'I've got enough explosives here to close this vault down for good. And enough money and tom outside in the tunnel to keep me in a way I could rapidly become accustomed to. Not as much as I anticipated, I agree, but I'm on my own now that George is dead. I'll take my chances.

And you'll be buried under a million tons of London.
How do you feel about that?'
   'You're bluffing.'
She laughed a horrible laugh. 'Try me,' she said.

Forty-four

I STAYED QUIET, lying there in the dark for a few minutes, trying to work out what to do for the best and coming up with not much, except for the .22 which I took out of the holster under my arm, but unless she put on some light I couldn't be sure of a shot the way her voice echoed around the vault so I couldn't know her exact location. Then she said, 'Well?'

'You're bluffing.'

'Try me.'

'You're serious?'

'Never more so.'

'Charming.'

'So what's it to be, Nick?'

'Looks like I don't have much choice,' I replied.

'I'm glad you see it that way,' she said.

'So how do we do this?'

'How many guns have you got?'

'A few.'

'How many's a few?'

'Enough,' I said, sliding the .22 back into its holster.

'Put on your torch.'

I did as I was told.

'Put it on its bottom and stand it upright.'

Once again I obeyed, but slowly. If she was going to shoot me down in cold blood, this would be the time.

'Put your guns on the floor.'

I did it. The empty Detonics, Finbarr's .38 and Billy's revolver.

'Walk to the wall and assume a position. You know the drill.'

I walked slowly to the nearest wall, put my hands on the surface at head height, walked back a step so that my hands took my weight and shuffled my feet apart.

I heard her footsteps behind me and she patted me down with one hand, the other keeping her gun at my neck. She found the .22 right away. It had only been a thought on my part. 'Tsk, tsk,' she said. 'You little liar.'

'You can't blame me for trying,' I said as she pulled it loose of the Velcro and put it into the back of her pants.

'Naughty boy,' she said, and let me have a good one with the end of the suppressor on her gun on the back of my head. 'Any more?'

I shook the aforementioned noggin.

She kept on frisking me, just making a faint sound of disgust when she touched my blood soaked shirt. 'Good,' she said when she was satisfied I was unarmed. 'Now, Nick, I hope you're not going to try anything else funny.'

'I won't.'

'I'd ask for your word but that's such a quaint, old-fashioned notion.'

'Look,' I said. 'I want to get out of here as much as you do. Let's get on with it.'

She stepped away and said, 'OK, let's do it.'

'Can I stand up straight now?' I asked.

'Sure.'

I caught my balance and turned. Her face was spooky in the light from the upturned torch. She still reminded me of Sheila but I no longer felt any attraction. I put my hand on the back of my head and in the light from the torch I saw blood.

'Put on that lantern,' she ordered.

I did as I was told using my lighter, and in the glow we could see the loot scattered about the floor, and the four bodies lying there with it. 'Jesus,' she said. 'Will you look at this.'

It certainly was a sight. Money and precious stones were scattered everywhere. 'Millions,' she whispered. 'Sodding millions.'

She was probably right. 'Let's have a look at that wound,' she said. 'I want you strong.'

I pulled up my blood-soaked sweatshirt and she had a squint. The blood was beginning to crust. I'd survive the wound to fight another day if the lovely Lucy let me. But the damned thing still hurt. 'Not too bad,' she said. 'Georgie's bag is by the hole. Fetch it.'

I did as I was told again and found a nylon bag just inside the entrance Morris had blown in the floor. 'Open it,' she said, and when I did I found all sorts of medical gear including field dressings. She made me slap one on the crease over my ribs and that helped. Once it was done, by the light of the lantern she collected the stray weapons, including my Detonics, and dropped them into Georgie's bag, which she stashed at the back of the vault.

'Right,' she said when she was done. 'Start packing up what's out in the open. Forget about the other boxes. There's enough here for us.'

I found a roll of the heavy duty garbage bags, split off one then another, folded the first into the second for extra strength, and started loading them with money and jewellery. Lucy hitched her backside on a pile of security drawers and sat and watched me work, her gun loose in her hand.

It took me almost an hour to pack up six bags of loot and stack them by the hole in the floor. There was no conversation as I worked, she just stayed sitting with the gun in her hand watching me, and the four dead bodies seemed to be watching me too.

Forty-five

EVENTUALLY SHE SAID, 'Now, the question is, can I trust you to take these bags out to Finbarr's office building?'

'So you know about that too,' I interrupted.

'I know about everything thanks to you,' she replied. 'Now as I was saying, can I trust you? Or foolish as it might be, would you just keep on going. Either to steal what's in the bags you take with you, or to go find a nice policeman and try to get me into trouble. And I don't mean land me with an unwanted baby. What do you say?'

I shrugged. 'Try me,' I said.

'That's precisely what I intend to do. I think you're more like me than you care to admit, Nick. And any other ways would be just too tiresome, like keeping you covered all the time or killing you. And I don't want to kill you. And besides, getting all the stuff out would be too hard on my body and clothes.' She looked down at her ruined jeans, muddy and torn, like mine from the journey in. 'But it'll be Prada from now on. Now that I don't have to rely on police wages. Anyway, enough of that. Let's not count our chickens. Where was I? Oh yes. So I'm just going to have to take a chance.' And with that she let down the hammer of her pistol and tucked it into the waistband of her jeans, this time at the front. 'Now how many bags can you manage at once, a big strong boy like you?'

'Four I suppose,' I replied. 'But that first tunnel's narrow, so the best thing for me to do is to take them through one at a time, pile them up at the other side and then carry them to the ladder.'

'I believe you're getting into the spirit of the thing, Nick,' she said. 'But before we do anything I have to make a few preparations.'

She sat me with my back against the wall, moved about

twenty yards away, then said, as if I hadn't worked it out for myself, 'If you try and run at me, I'll have plenty of time to get my gun out and shoot you. And you know I'm a good shot. Do you get me?'

'I do,' I said, and watched as she busied herself with some equipment.

'What are you doing?' I asked.

'This lot brought enough high explosive and bomb-making gear to start World War Three. I'm just borrowing it.'

'Do you know what you're doing?'

'In the army I worked in bomb disposal and then they sent me to demolition school. I know exactly what I'm doing.'

'A woman of many parts.'

'And most of them private, but yes, I've always thought it was advisable to have more than one string to my bow.'

When she was satisfied with her work she came back to join me. 'I'll explain exactly what's going to happen, Nick. I've prepared two bombs. One stays here and one comes with us. Both are on timers, the one coming with us will be set an hour after the first one. Like I said, there's a whole lot of HE in here. Far more than they needed, and when we're ready to go there'll be two big bangs that will seal the vault and the sewers.

'You're crazy.'

'Maybe. But they're just the kind of diversions we need to get away.'

'And then?'

'And then we ride away into the sunset together.'

'Really?'

'Really. It'll be good to have someone around to share this good fortune with.'

'And you've picked me.'

'You're big, not bad looking, you can satisfy me in bed if I decide to swing that way. You're quite amusing and you'll keep boring men away. Yes I think you'll do.'

'And what happens when you get tired of me?'

'I'm sure that will never happen.'

Who do you think you're kidding, I thought. You'll keep me around for just as long as it takes to get the loot away. Then it'll be shake 'n' bake time and you'll kill me.

But not if I kill you first.

Forty-six

B UT BEFORE ANY of that happened, I did as I'd been told yet again and pushed and pulled the bags of loot through the narrow tunnel, past the dead body of the bloke I'd stabbed, out into the main sewer, collecting the other bags as I went. It was awkward and it took time, but eventually I had the dozen bags of loot stacked neat as you please next to the river of dirty water where Finbarr still floated face down, and Lucy saved her manicure, although I can tell you it didn't do much for mine. By the time I was finished I was sweating like a pig and covered in muck from head to toe, and the sweat wasn't making my various wounds feel any better. 'You look a picture,' she said when I was done, and checked her watch. 'Look lively now, there's a bomb inside that vault, and it'll go off soon, and believe me we don't want to be down here when it does.'

'How long?' I asked.

'Long enough if you're quick.'

I said nothing in reply, just eased my aching muscles and wiped the sweat out of my eyes with the tail of my shirt.

'Right,' she said. 'Onward and upward. Grab as much as you can carry and let's get back to base.'

It took three trips, four bags a trip, bent almost double as the roof of the sewer dipped, but able to stand upright for the last part of each journey. Lucy kept me company but didn't lift as much as a diamond tiara, just kept hold of the second bomb she was carrying in Georgie's holdall.

'Up you go,' she said when everything was in place under the building where Finbarr had leased an office. 'Just push the bags through, no need to go through yourself.'

I did as I was ordered, taking a bag on each journey up the iron ladder and pushing it through the manhole at the top. It was dark in the corridor, and I thought I could smell moisture in the air.

Eventually my task was done and Lucy said, 'I'm going to set the timer on the second bomb.'

'Why bother to blow all this up too?' I asked.

'It'll cause another diversion,' she replied. 'They'll think the Irish are back in business.' She squatted down, pulled the bomb out of the bag and set to work. 'Shit,' she said after a minute. 'This timer's fucked. I'll have to go back.'

'Have we got time?' I asked.

'Plenty. Now do I have to handcuff you to that ladder?' she asked. 'Or are you going to wait here like a good boy?'

'I'll wait,' I said. After all the hard work I'd done I felt I was entitled to some reward. 'By the way, how do you figure to get all this stuff out of the area? There's a pretty big police presence outside you know.' And she should if anyone should, I thought. 'And plenty more once you start blowing holes in the landscape.'

'That's all taken care of. There's a van parked round the corner.'

'They let you park a van here? I thought the cops were all over parked vehicles like a rash.'

'It's a police van, love,' she replied sweetly.

'You think of everything.'

'I try.'

'I don't know, Nick,' she said, drawing her pistol. 'Something tells me you're being too helpful. I think maybe I should just make sure you don't make a run for it.' She took a set of cuffs from her pocket and under the gaze of the round mouth of the gun she cuffed me to one of the stanchions that held the ladder in place against the brick wall of the sewer, and with a cheerful wave made off back down the walkway, the light from her torch bobbing as she went.

I stood in the dark for what seemed like hours but in fact was only twenty minutes or so, with just the dim light from the open manhole above me bleeding into the blackness of the sewer. I tugged at the handcuff, but wobbly as the ladder was, it wouldn't give, so like a fool I left it.

Then I saw a light far away and eventually I recognised her. But something was different, the sewer was starting to run faster, and then from the opposite direction of Lucy's light I heard a strange sound that I couldn't immediately identify. Then I saw them. Loping down the far walkway were half a dozen skinny, mangy looking foxes who hardly paid me any attention as they ran past. Strange I thought.

Then there was another sound from the same direction that the foxes had come from. It was a patter, and a rustle, and a squeak that grew louder and louder and I squinted into the darkness trying to make out what it was, as a dark mass pinpricked with dots of red rushed towards me.

'What the fu –' I said, and the mass was upon me, and I realised it was a phalanx of rats streaming down the walkways on both sides of the sewer, rushing as fast as their little legs would carry them, away from I knew not what. It was a flesh and blood cohesion, as solid as a runaway truck, some of the rodents tumbling and turning somersaults in their panic to get away from what nameless terror was behind them. And as they hit me like a massive, furry fist, I turned away, and saw Lucy's terrified face just a few feet from mine, and then the rats were upon us, and I couldn't see anything for the multitude of them.

Forty-seven

'NICK,' SHE SCREAMED, and reached out her right hand which I grabbed with my left, my right being otherwise engaged with a pair of handcuffs, as the furry horde engulfed us. Her eyes were as full of fear as those of the rats that had come hopping and skipping down the sewer past us and heading in the direction that she'd arrived from, destination unknown. It seemed like hours that we were covered in them, their little feet catching on our clothes, their needle teeth nibbling at our extremities and their frightened squeals filling our ears, but in fact it could only have been a few seconds before they were gone. But the worst was yet to come. From the same direction as the rats I heard a roaring sound that was getting louder with every second, and I suddenly realised what was happening. Why the sewer water was running faster, and why the foxes and rats had fled. The weather forecast I'd heard on Finbarr's car radio on the way over had promised torrential storms in the London area, and if I was any judge, that was what was happening up top, and the sewers were filling. And filling bloody fast by the sound of it.

'The key,' I yelled to Lucy. 'Give me the key to the cuffs.'

'What?' she said.

'The bloody key. It's a flood.'

Recognition dawned on her face as the noise got louder, until my ears were almost filled with it, and she put down the bomb she was carrying and reached into her pocket for the slim piece of metal that would free me, but it was too late. The sewer echoed with the noise of rushing water, and the smell of moisture almost drowned out the smell of sewage, and as she pulled the handcuff key from her

pocket a solid wall of water came round the bend in the
sewer and hit us like a hammer.

I still had her hand in mine as we were both picked
up by the roiling waters and I could see the fear on her
face once more as her hand was torn from mine and she
disappeared in the torrent. 'Lucy,' I cried, but the words
were plucked from my mouth as the raging tide smashed
me against the wall, and all that I could think of was that
if I got through this I would be trapped down here cuffed
neatly to the ladder waiting for the cops to come pick
me up.

That was if I survived the bombs she'd set.

Forty-eight

THE TORRENT OF water seemed to grow stronger rather than decrease, and I was bodily lifted by the flow to a ninety degree angle, my nose, ears, eyes and mouth filling with liquid containing Christ knows what. I felt that my hand was about to be ripped from my arm as the cuff tightened, and I would have screamed with pain if I could have got my vocal chords to work. Jesus, I thought, I'm going to die here, but instead of my life flashing in front of my eyes, as I've heard happens, I could only imagine what the people who found me after the water had ebbed would make of a man dead by drowning, handcuffed to a stanchion in what would then be a dry sewer. Another bloody conundrum amongst so many recently. But then, just as I was beginning to lose consciousness, finally something on the rusty old ladder snapped and I was free and almost swept away by the flood as Lucy had been. The surprise shocked me back into the land of the living and luckily my fingers caught onto the vertical support of the ladder. I held on for dear life as gradually the current waned and I found my footing again, hardly able to breathe as I vomited water and muck from my nose and mouth.

After a minute I was able to let go of the ladder and kneel, bent almost double as I coughed up the last of the shit I'd swallowed and gradually got my breath back.

How long I stayed there on my knees I don't know, but the sewer water was still running fast when I eventually regained my feet and called out Lucy's name in a hoarse voice that didn't sound like my own.

But of her and the bomb she'd been carrying in Georgie's bag there was neither sight nor sound.

The bomb, I thought. Jesus. How long had she set the

detonator for? Not long I'd bet my life, and I didn't want
to be inside the sewer when it went off.

So, abandoning her to her fate, as she had abandoned
her sister and her girlfriend, I climbed the rickety ladder
for the last time and dropped the manhole cover back in
its grooves.

Bye bye Lucy I thought as it clanged shut. I hope you
rot in hell.

Forty-nine

I STOOD DRIPPING water like I'd just stepped out of a cold shower and looked round the corridor I was standing in, illuminated only by the dim glow from the lamps set in the ceiling, surrounded by the dozen bags of swag that I'd dragged from the vault, through the sewer and up the ladder. Now what the hell do I do with you lot? I thought. Outside there were cops and CCTV cameras everywhere and I didn't have the advantage of being able to use a police van as cover, as its exact whereabouts and ignition key had been washed away with Lucy. I looked at my watch. It said ten to three, but after all I'd been through I couldn't work out if it was morning or afternoon, or even exactly what day it was. I almost hit myself in the head to remember. Eventually I realised it must be Monday, but was it just starting or already half gone?

I shivered in the chill air, then kicked open the door to Finbarr's store room. The pile of clothes covered with dried mud was still where I remembered inside the windowless cube, and I sorted out a pair of trousers that were too big in the waist and too short in the leg, and a hooded sweatshirt that was far too small but would have to do. I pulled off my wet clothes and replaced them with the dry ones. The handcuffs were still hanging from my wrist and they could be a problem. I was never any good at picking locks, so I just took the free end and shoved it up the arm of the shirt. I could deal with that later. I took my wet clothes back into the corridor and dumped them in one of the bags.

I was standing there deciding what to do next when the first of Lucy's bombs went off. I heard a muffled boom, the whole building shook, the manhole cover danced a jig and the lights went out. 'Fire in the hole,' I whispered to myself.

I stood in the pitch dark so dense that I could almost hold it in my hand, and in the pocket of my leather jacket found my mini Maglite, which miraculously still worked after the soaking it had had. I said a silent thank you for American workmanship and headed up to the ground floor.

It was night, and I said another thank you for its cloak as I stumbled across the pitch black foyer of the building. The door was fastened by only a single Yale and I realised why Finbarr had chosen such an old building. The last thing he would've wanted was some modern job with a glass front and up-to-date security. I slipped the lock and pulled the door ajar and was immediately deafened by burglar alarms that had been set off by the explosion, and the roar of black rain onto the street. The roof of the world had slammed down like a trap door whilst I'd been underground. It was pouring, the heatwave had broken as promised and London was ground zero for a monsoon-like rainstorm. No wonder the sewers below had filled. It was dark outside also. Too dark, and for a second I couldn't work out why and then I realised. Not only had the building lights gone out, but the street lights were dead too. Lucy's bomb had blown the main electricity supply. Then from around a corner, blue lights and headlamps flashing, came a police car with its siren wailing. Gently I closed the front door but the cops went flying by. At least they weren't interested in me – yet.

I opened the door a crack again and was blinded by lightning that lit up the street and exposed a CCTV camera just opposite. In the afterburn of the flash I saw that its little red light was illuminated. Then the building was rocked again by the second bomb exploding somewhere down in the sewer system and a split second later it felt like a third had gone off, but I realised it was only the sound of thunder following the lightning. But Lucy's second bomb had done its job, and when I looked up at where the camera was mounted on the wall the red

light was out. That was my signal to pull the hood of
my sweatshirt over my head and sprint towards the car
park where Finbarr had parked his Jag, and for the first
time I thought I might just have a chance of getting
away clean.

I got to the car, found the keys under the mat where I'd
made him leave them, started it up, put on the full beams,
spun it round out of the parking bay and headed for the
exit. I tried using the ticket in the machine by the exit to
get me a pass out but it was dead, so I reversed the motor
as far back as it would go, slammed it into drive and with
a scream of rubber sped forward and smashed the gate
from its mooring, skidding out into the street and heading
back the way I'd come.

All the way the streets were empty, but I could hear
the ghostly screams of emergency vehicles echoing from
every building.

Fifty

I DROVE BACK through the pounding rain and parked, half on, half off the pavement in front of Finbarr's building. Naughty boy. I could get a ticket for that.

It had crossed my mind to leave the loot and do a runner, but after all I'd been through I thought that I deserved something for my trouble.

I opened the boot of the Jag. There was a lot of empty space in there which was handy for all the bags I had to carry, but that wasn't all. Nestling next to the spare wheel and tool kit was a pump action shotgun, sawn off fore and aft. It was black, short, ugly and frightening.

Shit, I thought. No wonder Fin had come over all peculiar when we were stopped by that female cop. If she'd asked him to pop the boot lid and seen that sitting there, God alone knows how it would all have worked out.

I left it, shut the lid and got busy.

It took four journeys to fill the boot to the brim. The rest would have to go in the back behind the front seats.

I only had one bad moment, when a crime car came creeping through the storm and slowed down next to me. Christ knows what I must've looked like, standing there, soaked to the skin, but as the window rolled slowly down I heard a voice on the car radio bark an order and the motor shot off, blues and twos full on. I can tell you I nearly pissed my pants.

I thought after that everything would be fine, but that just goes to show how wrong you can be.

Just as I'd finished loading the last bags and went back to see that I hadn't forgotten anything, as I was pulling the door shut behind me to leave everything neat and tidy, I saw that an unmarked car had stopped behind the Jag, only sidelights on, the sound of its engine muted by the rain. Two men got out of the front and waited for me at the foot of the short flight of stone steps leading from the front door to the pavement. 'Good evening, sir. Detective Constable Smart, City Police,' the one closest to me introduced himself, flashing a badge. 'Any problems here?'

'No constable,' I said. 'No problems at all. We're moving out.'

'Strange time,' said the other.

'Last knockings. Bank holiday weekend. Boss called me in. You know how it is.'

'No, sir,' said Smart. 'I don't. Didn't you hear the explosions?'

'Yes of course. All the lights went out. What happened?'

'We're not quite sure yet,' he replied. 'Bit hard to work in the dark?'

'Not really. It's just some bags of stuff. I had it all in the foyer.'

The rain beat down incessantly on our heads and ran down my back so that I shivered. But it wasn't just the cold water.

'Do you mind if we take a look?' asked the nameless cop.

'My pleasure,' I said, walked past them, keyed the lock on the Jaguar's boot, reached in, hauled out the shotgun and racked a shell into the breech. It would have been a joke on me if the gun had been empty but it wasn't.

'Turn round, both of you,' I ordered.

Their faces literally fell in the lights of their car. 'What's all this about?' said Smart.

'You'll find out.' I said. 'Maybe. If you're good and live that long. Now turn round. Don't look at me.'

They both did as they were told.

'Cuffs,' I said to their backs.

'What?' said Smart, half turning.

'Don't look at me,' I said. 'Cuffs and keys. Come on, even you City boys must make an arrest now and then.'

They did as I ordered, producing a pair of cuffs and a key each.

'Throw the keys away.'

They did.

'Smart. You handcuff your mate. Inside the railings.'

There was a tall, black iron fence in front of the building, the railings about six inches apart, joined at the top by another horizontal rail. Looked like it had been there for a hundred years and would last another hundred. The anonymous policeman stuck his hands through the railings and Smart put the bracelets on him so that it would take a metal cutter to free him.

'Put one on your right wrist,' I told Smart.

He did.

'Hands through,' I ordered.

Once more he obeyed.

Sticking the barrel of the shotgun under his chin one-handed, I awkwardly slapped the other cuff on his left hand. 'Don't look at me or try anything stupid,' I said as I did it.

He was as good as gold.

'Cheers chaps,' I said when they were both shackled. 'Sorry for the inconvenience.'

'You won't get away with this,' said the unnamed cop. 'Whatever it is.'

'That's right.'

'I think I just did,' I replied, and as I turned to go the crime car came drifting round the corner again.

Bloody hell I thought. This is most annoying, don't these fuckers ever take a tea break? And I walked out into the road and blew the radio aerial off the back of the motor.

I could see the driver's pale face through the windscreen, the wipers pushing the water out of the way, and I knew he was going to make a run for it, so I blew out the front tyre nearest to me, racked another shell into the breech and pointed the gun straight at him. 'No,' I screamed above the sound of the rain. 'Don't.'

Emotions rushed across his face in the next split second and I prayed I wouldn't have to shoot.

And I didn't. With a look of disgust he raised his hands off the steering wheel.

'Out,' I yelled, and the two uniforms in the car did so. 'On the fucking floor, and don't look at me.'

They both dropped to the sodden tarmac and raindrops bounced off the backs of their jackets.

'Personal radios,' I said. 'Get them off and throw them to me.'

Wisely, they did as they were told. It was all getting out of hand and could easily end in a bloodbath, which is the last thing I wanted.

I stamped on the radios until the plastic split and the guts were all over the street.

God knows how many shells the shotgun held. Could have been as few as three or as many as eight. Whatever. I just had to hope there were enough for what I wanted. I went to the passenger door and shot the shit out of the radio on the dash. Ditto with the plainclothes vehicle. That meant I'd fired four. I hoped I wouldn't need any more.

I left the coppers where they were and ran to the Jag, threw the shooter into the well by the passenger seat, jumped in, turned on the engine and sped off.

As I drove I wondered what the vault looked like after Lucy's bombs had gone off.

I reckoned there wasn't much left of it and as far as I was concerned the less the better.

I went to my garage and stored the gear in there, picked up a hacksaw, took one bag of cash and goodies up to my flat and stuck it under the bed with the saw on top, changed into some dry clothes that fitted, then took the Jag up to Crystal Palace, smashed it through the gates of an empty building site and set it on fire.

By then it had stopped raining, the skies had cleared

and the sun was rising. I threw the clothes I'd taken from
Finbarr's building into the flames and walked home, the
funeral pyre of the car painting the lavender sky black
behind me, and I heard the remaining shells in the shotgun
give me a salute as they exploded in the heat.

Once back at the flat I said hello to Teddy, sawed off
the handcuffs, showered, got dressed again and waited
for the cops to come as the story of what had happened
that weekend gradually unfolded on the TV news. Or at
least what they think happened.

Me and Teddy are still waiting.

EPILOGUE

O F COURSE THEY came.
    The cops that is. But not for a while.

Meantime I watched it all on prime time TV. What a show.

Lucy's bombs had decimated a great chunk of the City. The bank building had literally slid into its own foundations. There'd been nothing like it since the IRA bombed Docklands. It was the best free entertainment for years.

And then they discovered two bodies. Sergeant Lucille Madden of the Birmingham police and a solicitor from south London named Jerry Finbarr. Lucy had drowned and Finbarr had a bullet in his back. As far as I know they never found the weapon that killed him.

So the Bill rolled up onto my doorstep and asked me what I knew.

I denied everything, as you do, so they tugged me down to various police stations and I told my story a dozen times.

As far as I was concerned Lucy must've found out that Finbarr had something to do with the death of her sister and taken revenge. Why there, why then, why bombs I had no idea, but I must admit my palms were sweaty for a while.

Eventually they lost interest.

But not before they showed me some interesting footage of Finbarr walking through the area with another man on that Sunday. A man who kept his face hidden.

It could've been anyone, I said.

It could've been you, they said.

Prove it, I said.

Then they put me up in an ID parade and a pretty young female copper from a little village just outside Colchester took a squint.

No positive identification.

Nor from the other four police officers who came for a look. My God, I must've looked a state that night.

So as the summer turned to autumn to winter and the story went away, so did the coppers.

Eventually I took some of the money and put it into trust for my daughter.

I fenced a lot of the jewellery with someone I knew out of town. It helps to have friends in low places.

Then I booked myself a long holiday in a very warm place with no extradition treaty with the UK, and brought Teddy along for the ride.

It's very nice here, except for the mosquitoes that come out at night. They call them no-see-ums locally, because you can't. See them that is. Until it's too late.

But apart from that, the bars stay open all night, there's gambling at the casino, the sand is clean and white, the sea is clear and blue and they get the *Telegraph* just a few days late. And Teddy is a constant source of comfort.

Before I left I bought a couple of hundred quids' worth of red roses and drove them up to the cemetery and put them all around Sheila's grave, just like I promised I would. I didn't say much. There wasn't a lot to say.

So what do I do next?

I wish I knew.

ABOUT THE AUTHOR

In his almost twenty year writing career, Mark Timlin has written twenty-seven novels under six different names, innumerable short stories, including one anthology, plus articles on various subjects for various newspapers and magazines. He has made many friends, a few enemies, and had more laughs than two barrow loads of monkeys. His serial hero, Nick Sharman has appeared in a TV series for Carlton Television starring Clive Owen, only to be axed for excessive violence.

He is now the crime reviewer for *The Independent On Sunday*, lives in Docklands overlooking his beloved South London, drives a massive Lincoln Town Car, collects old vinyl, crime novels, and watches far too much daytime TV.

THE NO EXIT "18" ORDER FORM

___ 1842431498 **THE LEVANTER** Eric Ambler £ 6.99
___ 1842431501 **HAPPY BIRTHDAY, TURK!** Jakob Arjouni £ 6.99
___ 184243151X **BURGLAR WHO STUDIED SPINOZA** L. Block £ 6.99
___ 1842431528 **THE ANIMAL FACTORY** Edward Bunker £ 6.99
___ 1842431536 **LONDON BLUES** Tony Frewin £ 6.99
___ 1842431544 **FALLING ANGEL** William Hjortsberg £ 6.99
___ 1842431552 **NICE GIRLS FINISH LAST** Sparkle Hayter £ 6.99
___ 1842431560 **ALIVE & KICKING** John Milne £ 6.99
___ 1842431579 **TAPPING THE SOURCE** Kem Nunn £ 6.99
___ 1842431587 **WORD MADE FLESH** Jack O'Connell £ 6.99
___ 1842431595 **NIGHT PASSAGE** Robert B. Parker £ 6.99
___ 1842431609 **ANOTHER ROADSIDE ATTRACTION** T. Robbins £ 6.99
___ 1842431617 **DEATH WILL HAVE YOUR EYES** James Sallis £ 6.99
___ 1842431625 **PLEASE DON'T CALL ME HUMAN** Wang Shuo £ 6.99
___ 1842431633 **COLD CALLER** Jason Starr £ 6.99
___ 1842431641 **ALL THE EMPTY PLACES** Mark Timlin £ 6.99
___ 184243165X **MIAMI BLUES** Charles Willeford £ 6.99
___ 1842431668 **MUSCLE FOR THE WING** Daniel Woodrell £ 6.99

___ 1842431692 *NEP18* 256 pp First chapter/Crime Time SAMPLER Free

Name:

Address:

Postcode:

Credit Card Number:

Expiry Date: / **Issue No:**

Security Code (Last 3 digits on reverse of card by signature strip):

**All orders FREE P&P. Special offers: 3 books for £11.97,
5 books for £18, All 18 books for just £59.**

**Cheques payable in £Stg to Oldcastle Books Ltd.
Send Order to: No Exit Press, P O Box 394, Harpenden, AL5 1XJ**

No Exit Press, P O Box 394, Harpenden, AL5 1XJ, U.K.

T/F: Tel 0207 430 1021 Fax 0207 430 0021 www.noexit.co.uk/18